One of Barack Obama's Favourite Books of the Year

A National Book Award 5 Under 35 Honoree

Winner of the Center for Fiction First Novel Prize

'Leilani's story of Edie, a broke 23-year-old black woman who gets involved with a wealthy older white couple, cuts to the quick of the often grim realities of being young and black in the US today. But it's wincingly funny, too . . . Leilani's prose mesmerises; you go with her, wherever she decides to take you . . . A remarkable portrait of the artist as a young woman.'

Observer

'Written in cool prose as brittle as glass, *Luster* throws down the gauntlet to a politicised contemporary moment eager to see blazingly affirmative stories of black lives in literature . . . [Edie's] voice . . . is unforgettable. More novels like this please.'

Daily Mail

'You could stay in there all day, swathed in the magnificence of its language, the surprises of the sentences and their psychedelic, uncharted destinations . . . This is a book of pure fineness, exceptional.'

Diana Evans, *Guardian*

'So delicious that it feels illicit . . . Raven Leilani's first novel reads like summer: sentences like ice that crackle or melt into a languorous drip; plot suddenly, wildly flying forward like a bike down a hill.'

New York Times

'Every so often, a debut novel so dazzling in its brilliance renders you unable to see the world in quite the same way for some time. Raven Leilani's *Luster* illuminates the world anew, like a firework . . . it is truly a work of art.'

i

'This wild dark comedy is absolutely the real deal . . . Leilani's live-wire sentences are a giddy joy, crafted with mischievous perfection and full of smart things to say on hot-button issues.'

Mail on Sunday

'Raw, racy, and utterly mesmerizing, *Luster* is among the most dazzling novels of the year, marking the arrival of a major new voice . . . Dreamlike, tender, and big-hearted, *Luster* is a must-read.'

Esquire

'Darkly funny with wicked insight . . . This keenly observed, dynamic debut is so cutting, it almost stings.' *ELLE*

'With deadpan wit and remarkable talent, Raven Leilani effortlessly exposes the chasms between generations, faces and genders.'

Vogue

'*Luster* is ridiculously good: gorgeous, dark, and funny, with sentences that'll wreck you. I will follow this author anywhere she wants to take me.'

Carmen Maria Machado, author of *In the Dream House*

'*Luster* is a headlong carousel of a novel. With liquid prose and a painter's eye for colour, texture and light, *Luster* grapples vigorously with what it means to make art in a world pumping out racism-induced cortisol.'

Naoise Dolan, author of *Exciting Times*

'In this cutting, hot-blooded book, the entanglements that unfold are as complicated as they are heartbreaking.'

New Statesman

'Tension that keeps the reader hooked until the very last page . . . Leilani observes the dissatisfactions of Edie's 21st-century life with a brutal and beautiful keenness.' *Harper's Bazaar*

'If you like *Normal People*, you'll love *Luster* . . . a squirm-inducing marvel.'

BuzzFeed

'A coming-of-age story that's sure to keep you turning pages.'
Refinery29

'Spinning fresh commentary on both race and class, tensions in the house rise as Raven Leilani propels her lost protagonist on a darkly funny journey of self-discovery.'
Time

'A big, bold novel, visceral and unsettling, about a young Black woman desperate to find herself but looking in all the wrong places.'
Red magazine

'Brilliant in terms of voice, *Luster* is equally strong on plot and structure. In her leavening of cynicism with hope, Raven Leilani writes as if she were three books wise, at least.'
TLS

'This book is luminous, glorious. From the first sentence I knew there was word-magic here and that I would read any sentence Leilani cares to write. What a marvel.'
Daisy Johnson, author of *Everything Under*

'The narrative voice of this startling novel is layered, complex, pitch-black comic, and deadly earnest, even ardent in its will to sift through the chaos and idiocy of our madhouse culture and find some glimpse of human reality. Raven Leilani has made a truly lustrous piece of art.'
Mary Gaitskill, author of *This Is Pleasure*

'Raven Leilani's style is a truly original mix of the new and the wise, of wit and despair. She has poignantly captured the obsession that drives, and often destroys, every true artist. I adored *Luster* for its honesty and weird beauty.'
Sara Baume, author of *Spill Simmer Falter Wither*

'I adored this wry, vital, mesmeric novel. In glorious, exhilarating sentences, Leilani crafts a story that is both deeply moving and brimming with originality and insight.'
Megan Hunter, author of *The Harpy*

'A beguiling fever dream of a novel, shot through with wistfulness, humor, and a kind of breathless, furious verve. You'll find it impossible to put down.'

Ling Ma, author of *Severance*

'Hilarious, honest, bursting with desire and cutting insight, *Luster* is absolutely captivating. I didn't so much read it, as gulp it down. There's so much to learn here, so much to admire. Leilani is an irreverent, impeccable stylist—a voice we need right now.'

Justin Torres, author of *We the Animals*

'*Luster* is as close to perfect a book as you'll read this year. I promise you – Raven Leilani is about to become your new obsession.'

Louise O'Neill, author of *Asking For It*

'Raven Leilani is a writer of unusual daring, with a voice that is unique and fully formed. There is humor, intelligence, emotion, and power in her work. I cannot think of a writer better suited to capture our contemporary moment.'

Katie Kitamura, author of *A Separation*

LUSTER

Raven Leilani's work has been published in *Granta*, *McSweeney's Quarterly Concern* and *The Cut*, among other publications. Leilani received her MFA from NYU and is currently the Axinn Foundation Writer in Residence there. *Luster* is her first novel.

LUSTER

RAVEN LEILANI

PICADOR

First published 2020 by Farrar, Straus and Giroux, New York

First published in the UK in paperback 2020 by Picador

This edition first published 2021 by Picador
an imprint of Pan Macmillan
The Smithson, 6 Briset Street, London EC1M 5NR
EU representative: Macmillan Publishers Ireland Ltd, 1st Floor,
The Liffey Trust Centre, 117–126 Sheriff Street Upper,
Dublin 1, D01 YC43
Associated companies throughout the world
www.panmacmillan.com

ISBN 978-1-5290-3600-8

3 5 7 9 8 6 4 2

A CIP catalogue record for this book is available from the British Library.

Printed and bound by CPI Group (UK) Ltd, Croydon, CR0 4YY

MIX
Paper from
responsible sources
FSC® C116313

Visit www.picador.com to read more about all our books
and to buy them. You will also find features, author interviews and
news of any author events, and you can sign up for e-newsletters
so that you're always first to hear about our new releases.

For my mother

LUSTER

1

The first time we have sex, we are both fully clothed, at our desks during working hours, bathed in blue computer light. He is uptown processing a new bundle of microfiche and I am downtown handling corrections for a new Labrador detective manuscript. He tells me what he ate for lunch and asks if I can manage to take off my underwear in my cubicle without anyone noticing. His messages come with impeccable punctuation. He is fond of words like *taste* and *spread*. The empty text field is full of possibilities. Of course I worry about IT remoting into my computer, or my internet history warranting yet another disciplinary meeting with HR. But the risk. The thrill of a third pair of unseen eyes. The idea that someone in the office, with that sweet, post-lunch-break optimism, might come across the thread and see how tenderly Eric and I have built this private world.

In his first message, he points out a few typos in my online profile and tells me he has an open marriage. His profile pictures are candid and loose—a grainy photo of him asleep in the sand, a photo of him shaving, taken from behind. It is this last photo that moves me. The dirty tile and the soft recession of steam. His face in the mirror, stern with quiet scrutiny. I save the photo to my phone so I can look at it on the train. Women look over my shoulder and smile, and I let them believe he is mine.

Otherwise, I have not had much success with men. This is not a statement of self-pity. This is just a statement of the facts. Here's a fact: I have great breasts, which have warped my spine. More facts: My salary is very low. I have trouble making friends, and men lose interest in me when I talk. It always goes well initially, but then I talk too explicitly about my ovarian torsion or my rent. Eric is different. Two weeks into our correspondence, he tells me about the cancer that ravaged half of his maternal family. He tells me about an aunt he loved who made potions with fox hair and hemp. How she was buried with a corn husk doll she'd made of herself. Still, he describes his childhood home lovingly, the digressions of farmland between Milwaukee and Appleton, the yellow-breasted chats and tundra swans that would appear in his yard, looking for seed. When I talk about my childhood, I only talk about the happy parts. The VHS of *Spice World* I received for my fifth birthday, the Barbie I melted in the microwave when no one was home. Of course, the context of my childhood—the boy bands, the Lunchables, the impeachment of Bill Clinton—only emphasizes our generational gap. Eric is sensitive about his age and about mine, and he makes a considerable effort to manage the twenty-three-year discrepancy. He follows me on Instagram and leaves lengthy comments on my posts. Retired internet slang interspersed with earnest remarks about how the light falls on my face. Compared to the inscrutable advances of younger men, it is a relief.

We talk for a month before our schedules align. We try to meet earlier, but things always come up. This is just one way his life is different from mine. There are people who count on him, and sometimes they need him urgently. Between his abrupt cancellations, I realize that I need him, too. In a way that makes my dreams delirious expressions of thirst—long stretches of yellow desert, cathedrals hemmed in dripping moss. By the time we set our first real date, I would've done anything. He wanted to go to Six Flags.

We decide to go on a Tuesday. When he rolls up in his white Volvo, I have only made it to the part of my pre-date routine where I try to find the most appropriate laugh. I put on three dresses before I find the right one. I tie up my braids and line my eyes. There are dishes in the sink and a pervasive salmon smell in the apartment, and I don't want him to think it has anything to do with me. I put on a complex pair of underwear that is not so much underwear as a bundle of string, and I stand before the mirror. I think to myself, *You are a desirable woman. You are not a dozen gerbils in a skin casing.*

Outside, he is double-parked. He leans against the car and remains like this as I come out, his eyes bright and still. His hair is darker than I expected, a black so opaque it looks blue. His face is almost obscenely symmetrical, though one of his eyebrows is higher than the other, and it makes his smile seem a little smug. It is the second day of summer and all the city's powers have no sway over him. I reach for his hand, trying not to swallow my tongue, and something feels strange. Of course there are nerves. In person he is a total daddy, his face alert and hard, softened only by the slight recession of his hair. But this strange feeling has nothing to do with that, nothing to do with me looking past his sensuous mouth and slightly askew nose for any indication that he is as nervous as I am. It is that it is 8:15 a.m. and I feel happy. I am not on the L, smelling someone's lukewarm pickles, wishing I were dead.

"Edie," I say, extending my hand.

"I know," he says, his long fingers settling between mine, too gently. I wanted to be more forward, to fold him into an easy, extroverted hug. But what happens is this limp handshake, this aversion of my eyes, this unsurprising and immediate surrender of power. And then the worst part of meeting a man in broad daylight, the part where you see him seeing you, deciding in this split second whether any future cunnilingus will be enthusiastic or perfunctory. He opens the door, and there is a fluffy blue die hanging from the rearview mirror. A half-eaten bag of Jolly Ranchers in the passenger seat. His correspondence online has been honest, full of his stuttering sincerity. However, as we have already told the stories you might tell on a first date, it is harder to begin. He brings up the weather and then we are talking about climate change. After a while of talking generally about burning to death, we pull into the park.

———

It's hard not to be aware of an age discrepancy when you are surrounded by the most rococo trappings of childhood. The Tweety Bird balloons, the plastic, soulless eyes of the Taz mascot, the Dippin' Dots. As we enter the gates, I feel the high-fructose sun of the park like an insult. This is a place for children. He has taken me to a place for children. I watch his face for any indication that this might be a joke or a telling manifestation of his anxiety about the mere twenty-three years I've spent on earth.

The age discrepancy doesn't bother me. Beyond the fact of older men having more stable finances and a different understanding of the clitoris, there is the potent drug of a keen power imbalance. Of being caught in the excruciating limbo between their disinterest and expertise. Their panic at the world's growing indifference. Their rage and adult failure, funneled into the reduction of your body into gleaming, elastic parts.

Except, for him, this seems to be new territory. Not simply to be out on a date with someone who is not his wife and decades younger, but to be out with a girl who happens to be black. I can feel it in how cautiously he says *African American*. How he absolutely refuses to say the word *black*. As a rule, I try to avoid popping that dusky cherry. I cannot be the first black girl a white man dates. I cannot endure the nervous renditions of backpacker rap, the conspicuous effort to be colloquial, or the smugness of pink men in kente cloth. As we make our way over to the lockers, a father and son are vomiting behind a Bugs Bunny standee. I open my locker and there is a diaper inside. Eric sees it and calls over a janitor. Eric says he's sorry, and the apology feels like it is not about only the diaper, but more how this choice of location is turning out. I feel bad about that. I feel bad that my first instinct is to manage his feelings, instead of suggesting somewhere else to go. That we will both have to endure my attempt to prove over the course of this date that I Am Having a Good Time! and that This Is Not Your Fault!

A month is too long to talk online. In the time we have been talking, my imagination has run wild. Based on his liberal use of the semicolon, I just assumed this date would go well. But everything is different IRL. For one thing, I am not as quick on my feet. There is no time to consider my words or to craft a clever response in iOS Notes. There is also the fact of body heat. The inarticulable parts of being close to a man, the sweet, feral thing underneath their cologne, the way it sometimes feels as if there are no whites to their eyes. A man's profound, adrenal craziness, the tenuousness of his restraint. I feel it on me and in-side me, like I am being possessed. When we talked online, we both did some work to fill in the blanks. We filled them in opti-mistically, with the kind of yearning that brightens and distorts. We had elaborate, hypothetical dinners and we talked about the doctor's appointments we were afraid to make. Now there are no blanks, and when he rubs sunblock on my back, it is both too little and too much.

"Is this okay?" he asks, his breath hot on the back of my neck.

"Uh-huh," I say, trying not to make the contact into more than it is. However, his hands are excellent. They are warm and wide and soft, and I have not been laid in months. For a moment, I'm sure I'm going to cry, which is not unusual, because I cry often and everywhere, and most especially because of this one Olive Garden commercial. I excuse myself and run to the bathroom, where I look into the mirror and reassure myself that there are bigger things than the moment I am in. Gerrymandering. Genealogy conglomerates selling my cheek swabs to the state.

Of course, there is still the business of trying to look sexy while hurtling across the sky. Like most white people who eat beans in the woods undeterred by the fresh fecal evidence of hungry bears, Eric finds his mortality and soft meaty body a petty, incidental thing. I, on the other hand, am acutely aware of all the ways I might die. So when the sighing teenage park associate slaps my harness down and slogs over to the levers, I think of all my unfinished business—the quart of pistachio gelato in my freezer, the 1.5 wanks left in my half-dead vibrator, my *Mister Rogers* box set.

Eric's enthusiasm is infectious. After the first two rides, I am enjoying myself, and not just because dying means I won't have to pay my student loans. He laces his fingers into mine and drags me to the front, apparently serious enough about his park experience to have paid the extra fee to skip the line. I go to tie my shoelaces and return to find him talking to the Porky Pig mascot about entry-level positions at the archive.

"We always need quality customer service," he says, pressing his phone number into Porky's pink felt mitt. We board the highest coaster in the park for the third time and he screams like it is the first. He really, truly screams. At first it is off-putting, but as we scale the last track, I realize that I like it. I like it a lot. I can't decide if it's the dissonance, the girliness of this inclination compared to his mass, or my envy of his wonder—the glee in his terror, the willingness to experience anew what is familiar. His joy is raw in a way that makes me feel like I can unzip my skin suit and show him all the ooze inside. But not yet. There is a sadness about his fervor, the way it feels slightly put on, as if he has something to prove. He looks over at me when we reach the top. The wind cards through his hair. Behind his eyes, I see myself fractured into pieces. Suddenly it feels painful to be this ordinary, to be this open to him, as he looks at me and pretends I am not just a cheaper version of a fast Italian car.

"I wish every day could be like this," he says when we reach the most terrifying part of the ride, when they hold you in midair and force you to anticipate the drop. Below us, the park is turning on its lights. All I want is for him to have what he wants. I want to be uncomplicated and undemanding. I want no friction between his fantasy and the person I actually am. I want all that and I want none of it. I want the sex to be familiar and tepid, for him to be unable to get it up, for me to be too open about my

IBS, so that we are bonded in mutual consolation. I want us to fight in public. And when we fight in private, I want him to maybe accidentally punch me. I want us to have a long, fruitful bird-watching career, and then I want us to find out we have cancer at exactly the same time. Then I remember his wife, the coaster eases downward, and we fall.

Despite myself, I have been thinking about his wife all day. I find myself hoping she is a vocal participant in her neighborhood watch. It would also be reassuring if she lies completely still during sex. There is the possibility that she might be cool. She might truly be fine with her husband going out on a date with a girl who has sixteen times more viable eggs. She might be limber, keyed into Venus retrograde, and inclined to use natural deodorant. A woman so unthreatened by all of New York's women that she has given this nubile horde a wholesale blessing to fuck her husband.

After a few more rounds, Eric and I head to a faux saloon with a surprising abundance of wicker. It is the one restaurant in the park allowed to sell alcohol, and above the bar is a neon rendition of Yosemite Sam's handlebar mustache. A waitress wearing a ten-gallon hat tosses a couple of sticky menus on the table. She tells us the specials in such a way that we know our sole responsibility as patrons in her section is to just go right ahead and fuck ourselves. Up until this moment, we have been riding through the day side by side. I look at him directly and it almost hurts. His undivided attention is like a focused point of heat.

"Are you having a good time?" he asks.

"Yeah, I think so."

"Because I have to be honest, I'm having trouble reading you, and I'm usually great at that kind of thing." I finish my beer and try not to show how overjoyed I am that none of my need and loathing have come across. "You're kind of aloof," he says, and all the kids stacked underneath my trench coat rejoice. Aloof is a casual lean, a choice. It is not a girl in Bushwick, licking clean a can of tuna.

"I'm an open book," I say, thinking of all the men who have found it illegible. I made mistakes with these men. I dove for their legs as they tried to leave my house. I chased them down the hall with a bottle of Listerine, saying, *I can be a beach read, I can get rid of all these clauses, please, I'll just revise.*

So I do my best to be unimpressed. For as long as I can, I try to make it look like my silence is discerning, as opposed to being fearful of what embarrassing thing I might say.

"Are you dating anyone else?" he asks.

"No. Does that make you want me less?"

"No, does me being married make you want me less?"

"It makes me want you more," I say, wondering if I'm beginning to say too much, if it was a mistake to tell him that he is the only one. No one wants what no one wants. There is a pervasive weed-bathroom-popcorn smell in the air, and a man at the bar is quietly crying next to a giant teddy bear. For the first time it occurs to me that Eric might've chosen this location to ensure that we didn't run into anyone he knows in the city. "I liked it when you asked if I was having a good time," I say.

"Why?" He frowns, and I realize I have seen this one before, that after a few hours his facial expressions are already becoming familiar to me. When I think of how we will only move forward from here, how we will never return to the relative anonymity of the internet, I want to fold myself into a ball. I hate the idea that I have repeated an action, that he has looked at me, discerned a pattern, and silently decided whether it is something he can bear to see again. There is nothing I can do to level the playing field. Some men at least have the decency to guide you immediately to all the things that are wrong with them. But everything I've seen of Eric, I want to see again. Like this vaguely paternal old man frown, his gentle disapproval.

"Because I felt you were really waiting for my answer, that it wasn't one of those questions you ask because you expect the answer to be yes," I say.

"Give me an example of a question like that."

"Here's one: Did you come?"

"And so you say yes, even if the answer is no?"

"Of course."

"Well, you're just a little liar, aren't you?" he says, and I want to say, *Yes. Yes, I am.*

"You don't ever lie to spare feelings?"

"Never."

"Interesting," I say. Of course, it is not interesting that he has been allowed to live candidly. It is not interesting that he cannot conceive of anything else. He has equated his range of motion with mine. He hasn't considered the lies you tell to survive, the kindness of pretend, which I illustrate now, as I eat this bacterial hot dog. This is the first time I sort of understand him. He thinks we're alike. He has no idea how hard I'm trying.

"You can be yourself with me, you know," he says, and it's all I can do not to laugh right in his face.

"Thanks," I say, but I know he doesn't mean it. He wants me to be myself like a leopard might be herself in a city zoo. Inert, waiting to be fed. Not out in the wild, with tendon in her teeth.

"Also, if I don't make you come, I want you to tell me," he says, motioning for the check.

"So we're going to have sex? This is going well?"

"Don't you think so?"

On our way back to the car, it begins to rain. The rain is light but unexpected, and the park is already halfway through the closing fireworks. We stand in the lot and wait for the finale. He drapes his arm around me as they start to send up the white dahlias. I press my face into his shirt, and it is damp with sweat and chlorine. All day it has been impossible to get dry. He touches the back of my neck and his fingers stick.

When we get in the car, the windows are wet on our side of the glass. He turns on the wipers and removes his shirt. He has this smile as he does it that gives me the impression he is aware of himself, and it makes me want to sit on his face. I have prepared for this. I wore this dress because it is easy to take off. But then he puts the car in drive and we are on the road. I sit and watch the roadside lights strobe across his face. The route from Jersey to the city is unusually clear. He hangs his arm out of the window and sings along to the radio in a soft, confident voice. The song on the radio is Idris Muhammad's "Could Heaven Ever Be Like This." It came out in 1977, three years after Eric was born. I sing along in the least weird way I can manage, which is still pretty weird.

"How do you know this?" he says, and I want to be cool. I want to say that I found the record in a shop, misplaced behind some goblin prog. Not that I heard it sampled by two separate songs and spent 2003–2006 on crude message boards, trying to seek it out. I want to tell him that Donna Summer's "Spring Affair" is the only thing that got me through 2004, but I have omitted the events of this year from our correspondence.

"I love disco," I say, and he smiles and turns up the music. This is how we travel into the city, aloft on the late seventies. He drives at a mellow clip with one hand on the wheel, and I know I am almost home when the air begins to stink. When we pull up to the curb, he turns down the music and asks again if I had a good time.

"Yes," I say, my ears still full of the highway wind.

"You better not be lying to me," he says, and then his hand is on my thigh. Wrapped around the back of my neck. There is no discernible pattern to his touch and he is so silent I can't even hear him breathing. Otherwise, I am aware of every atmospheric fluctuation inside the car: the lost radio channel and low FM fuzz, half in half out, so that against the lazy circles of his fingers a voice occasionally emerges from the speaker with oily DJ verve and says *you're listening to*; the dome light; the dim halo around his head; his eyes large and bright.

"I want you to suck my fingers," he says.

"Okay," I say, and take one finger into my mouth. And then two. And then three. And then suddenly, he hooks his fingers and pulls me toward him by the bottom row of my teeth.

"You fucking slut," he says, and then releases me.

"Come up."

"Not tonight. Let me take you out on Thursday."

"Sure," I say, but I am embarrassed. All day I have been waiting to take him apart. I cleaned my room and bought three boxes of Plan B. I get out of the car and wave as he drives away. As I climb the stairs to my apartment, I have already resolved to call out of work tomorrow and spend all night furiously masturbating to *Top Chef*.

Unfortunately, my vibrator is dead. I scrounge around for some batteries, but none of the ones I find are double-A. I try to use my fingers, but a roach crawls across the ceiling when I'm getting close. When I look in the mirror, one of my falsies is gone. I hope this has happened recently, and I have not been walking around all day with one sad, glue-drenched eye. Everything I've done to prepare for his visit feels embarrassing. The extra toothbrush, the eggs and LaCroix I bought for our postcoital brunch. I make an omelet and eat it in the dark. I think of the look on his face when he had his fingers in my mouth. His sneer, suspended in the blue-dark.

———

I look for my paints, and when I find them, they are mostly congealed. It has been two years since I painted anything, but I have optimistically kept a bag of art supplies on hand. There is a dead mouse in the bag, and I have no idea how long it's been in there. Because for two years I have slowly moved all my art supplies out of view. I have woken up from dreams where my hands are slick with oil and turpentine and lost the inspiration by the time I brushed my teeth. The last time I painted, I was twenty-one. The president was black. I had more serotonin and I was less afraid of men. Now the cyan and yellow come out hard. I need hot water to make them mix. I work with the paint, let the acrylic dry, and when it isn't right I rework it again. I remain as faithful as I can to scale. I mix thirteen shades of green, five shades of purple I don't need. My palette knife breaks in two. When it is almost 5:00 a.m., I have a passable replication of Eric's face. The slope of his nose in the soft red light of the dash. I rinse my brushes and watch dawn come in its smoky metropolitan form. Somewhere in Essex County, Eric is in bed with his wife. It's not that I want exactly this, to have a husband or home security system that, for the length of our marriage, never goes off. It's that there are gray, anonymous hours like this. Hours when I am desperate, when I am ravenous, when I know how a star becomes a void.

On Thursday morning the hot water isn't running and there is a new mouse caught in the trap. My roommate and I have been supporting a family of mice for six months. We have gone through a series of traps and yelled at each other in Home Depot about what constitutes a humane death. My roommate wanted to bomb the place, but none of our windows open. So we have these plain glue traps that are engineered to smell like peanut butter. The thing is, to unstick the mouse I have to go outside and pour canola oil on its feet. Yes, there are always tunnels in my bread. Yes, my landlord, a twenty-three-year-old Flat Tummy Tea Instagram shill who inherited the building from her grandfather, is ignoring my emails. But we are all trying to eat. So when I'm outside trying to release this distressed, balding mouse while the fat calico is watching from the deli across the street, it's like this mouse infestation and I are in it together. When I go back inside, I think about how little the mouse wants. I think about the chicken grease and peanut butter. I think about how before lunchtime, one of the bodega cats will rise from a crate of Irish Spring and welcome the mouse into its jaws.

Inside I throw on my least wrinkled dress. I look into the mirror and practice my smile, because they moved me to a desk where my manager can see my face, and I have noticed her growing concern. Management claims they moved me so that I am more accessible to staff, but I know it is because of Mark. My first two years on the job, I sat in the outer limits of the office, where the children's imprint transitions into epub-only romance. There, I was fortunate enough to face a wall, where I could blow my nose privately. Now I am social. I show my teeth to my coworkers and feign surprise at the dysfunction of the MTA. There is a part of me that is proud to be involved in these small interactions, which confirm that I am here and semi-visible and that New York is squatting over other people's faces too, but another part of me is sweating through the Kabuki, trying to extend my hand and go off script.

I have about ten hours until my date with Eric, which means I have to eat as little as possible. I cannot anticipate the overreactions of my stomach, so if I think there is even the slightest possibility of sex, I have to starve. Sometimes the sex is worth it and sometimes it's not. Sometimes there is a premature ejaculation and it is 11:00 p.m. and I have twenty minutes to make it to the closest McDonald's with an intact ice cream machine. I pack a can of black olives for lunch. I roll on some lipstick, hoping the maintenance of the color will make me less inclined to eat.

By the time I push my way onto the train, the sun is nuking all the garbage in Manhattan. We stall for traffic at Montrose, Lorimer, and Bedford, and the dark tunnel walls make mirrors of the windows. I turn away from my reflection and a man is masturbating under a tarp. I almost lose a seat to a woman who gets on at Union Square, but luckily her pregnancy slows her down. I arrive at work eighteen minutes late, and the editorial assistants are already directing the wave of phone calls to publicity.

I am the managing editorial coordinator for our children's imprint, meaning I occasionally tell the editorial assistants to fact-check how guppies digest food. I call meetings where we discuss why bears are over, and why children only want to read about fish. The editorial assistants do not invite me to lunch. I try to be approachable. I try to understand my group of pithy nihilists who all hail from the later end of Gen Z. There is only one EA I try to avoid, and this is the one who comes first thing this Thursday morning to my new, centrally located desk.

"I don't know how these reporters are getting our direct lines. Have you seen Kevin?" Aria is the most senior editorial assistant. She is also the only other black person in our department, which forces a comparison between us that never favors me. Not only is she always there to supply a factoid that no one knew about Dr. Seuss, she is also lovely. Lovely like only island women are; her skin like some warm, synthetic alloy. So she's very popular around the office with her reflective Tobagonian eyes and apple cheeks, doing that unthreatening aw-shucks shtick for all the professional whites. She plays the game well, I mean. Better than I do. And so when we are alone, even as we look at each other through borrowed faces, we see each other. I see her hunger, and she sees mine.

"I don't know, maybe Kevin was finally beamed up by the Heritage Foundation," I say, taking my coffee into my hand.

"This isn't a joke to me," she says. For the most part I've stopped worrying that she is compiling a list of reasons she should have my job, because now it is not a question of whether she will take my job, it is a question of when. The only thing that bothers me is that I still want to be her friend. On her first day, she came into the office meek and gorgeous, primed to be a token. And as you are wont to do—having always been the single other in the room, having somehow preserved hope that the next room might be different—she looked around, searching for me. When she found me, when we looked at each other that first time, finally released from our respective tokenism, I felt incredible relief.

And then I miscalculated. Too much anger shared too soon. Too much can you believe these white people. Too much fuck the police. We both graduated from the school of Twice as Good for Half as Much, but I'm sure she still finds this an acceptable price of admission. She still rearranges herself, waiting to be chosen. And she will be. Because it is an art—to be black and dogged and inoffensive. She is all these things and she is embarrassed that I am not.

I'd like to think the reason I'm not more dogged is because I know better. But sometimes I look at her and wonder if the problem isn't her, but me. Maybe the problem is that I am weak and overly sensitive. Maybe the problem is that I am an office slut.

"They're never going to give you the power you want," I say because I'm jealous, and it is interesting how she wavers between her mask and this offering of conspiracy. She leans down and there it is, that sweet, copyrighted black girl smell—jojoba oil, pink lotion, blue magic.

"How would you know? You're still a managing editorial co-ordinator, and you've been here three years," she says, and I could assert my seniority, but that would be embarrassing. The difference in our entire yearly salaries is one monthly student loan payment.

"We just got a bunch of proofs for that series we're doing on bath time. Can you take care of those?" I say, turning away from her. I check my phone, hoping there might be a text from Eric. Some reassurance that our first date truly went well, or some indication that he is excited about tonight. I think about sending him a comprehensive list of things he is allowed to do to me, so that we are on the same page, but when I have a draft, it has kind of a Helga Pataki vibe. I try my hand at it a few more times before I give up and go to find Kevin, who has acquired the book at the center of this PR nightmare, an illustrated history for the conservative child, a lyrical meditation on the radicalism of the liberal media and the martyrdom of rural states.

If I have to be objective, the art in this book is something. The moody gouache sunsets over Confederate camp. Lincoln's saggy thought bubble as he looks into the future, disappointed by the state of his party. The photorealistic depictions of urban crime. I find Kevin walking around his office in one sock, talking on the phone as this G-rated agitprop flies off the shelves. And then I see Mark. I'm not proud of what I do then, which is duck into the stairwell and hold my breath. Of all the men I've slept with at work, this is the one who cost me the most. What they say about not shitting where you eat only holds if they pay you enough to eat. For the most part, this has been the best part of the job.

Onboarding with Mike, his little fingers and junior human resources lingo as I cajole him out of his pants. Jake from IT coming up the stairs at 6:00 p.m. with his key fob, breathing on my neck about admin privileges while he addresses the service desk ticket about my broken monitor. Hamish from contracts in the nursing room with that blue streak in his hair and his hairy thighs asking me so sweetly if I could call him *Lord*. Tyler, managing editor of lifestyle and self-help, his fanned glossies and sock garters, pushing my head down while he's on the phone with the Dublin office. Vlad from the mailroom with his broken

English and all the packing peanuts around us on the floor. Arjun from the British sales group with his slick black hair and cartoon villain forearms, all riled up by Scholastic poaching high performers on his team. Jake from IT, again, because these computers are shit and he has the prettiest dick I've ever seen. Tyrell from production with his halfway smile in the bathroom stall at the office Christmas party, string lights a fractal echo in his dark, reflective eyes. Michelle from legal sitting on the copier, nylons slung around her neck as fluorescents flicker overhead. Kieran from bodice rippers taking me from behind and going on and on about severing my body from my limbs and the whole time I'm laughing and I don't know why. Jerry who is acquiring all the cancer-centric YA, making bank and soft love to me in the conference room with the aerial view of 30 Rock and I'm crying and I don't know why. Joe from true crime who doesn't read at all and who comes loud and quick and calls me *nigger* and then *mommy*. Jason from STEM textbooks who wants me to cry just like I did for Jerry, which is an experience I do cry about, at home. Adam from Christian erotica coming on my face and I feel nothing. And then Jake, one more time, because my keyboard is on the fritz, but it isn't Jake but John from IT who comes, sliding his hand beneath my shirt, telling me that Jake was in a bad car accident and it isn't looking good.

And somewhere in between, Mark. Mark, head of the art department, where the air smells like warm paper and everyone is happy. Where there are silky sheaves of eighteen-by-twenty-four and the printers are sighing in self-generated heat, churning out deep blacks and liquid blues like clockwork, panels as clear as water, so saturated that if you touch it fresh you can feel the wet. The people in the art department move around the building in smiling clusters, concept work cradled in their arms. They have passionate debates in the elevator about embossing and Verdana and Courier New. They have their own hours and their own dress code, each in that chic, dorky limbo that is the domain of the old art school kid. And all I want is to be one of them. I want to order takeout from the dumpling house across the street and stay in the office until ten, revising the vista behind Frank the Fox from ultramarine to cerulean to cyan. I have applied three times. I have interviewed twice. And in both cases they have asked me to do more work on my basic figure drawing skills. Mark told me that they would keep my résumé on file, and so I went and flunked some night classes I could not afford, thwarted by the dimples in human muscle and especially by the metatarsal bones in the foot. I stuck to graphite and paper, hoping that unlike paint, the medium would afford me more control, but my figures kept blurring under the heel of my hand.

When it comes to this, I cannot help feeling that I am at the end of a fluctuation that originated with a single butterfly. I mean, with one half degree of difference, everything I want could be mine. I am good, but not good enough, which is worse than simply being bad. It is almost. The difference between being there when it happens and stepping out just in time to see it on the news. Still, I can't help feeling that in the closest arm of the multiverse, there is a version of me that is fatter and happier, smiling in my own studio, paint behind my ears. But whenever I have tried to paint in the last two years, I have felt paralyzed.

And Mark is not exactly pressed against the chapel ceiling or projecting this bleached, Warholian cool. He is a grown man in a duster who keeps fresh orchids in his office, collects polymer toys, and does Groening-esque renditions of *The Dream of the Fisherman's Wife*. And one day it was raining and 8:00 p.m., and he and I shared an elevator. He showed me a panel of a cunnilingual octopus, and the care he had taken to render this piece knocked me right over and onto his cock. But it isn't like the others—the ecstatic rutting and cushy ether of the void. It is like I really need him. Because there are men who are an answer to a biological imperative, whom I chew and swallow, and there are men I hold in my mouth until they dissolve. These men are often authority figures. And so Mark was very kind, taking me out and deepening my palate and ordering all the wine. He took me back to his apartment, the sort of New York real estate that seems impossible, lousy with light and square footage like some telegenic Hollywood lie.

The sex is okay but sort of beside the point, because in his drawing room there are buckets of Prismacolors, Copic markers, and oils. Rolls of raw canvas, cans of lumpy gesso and turpentine. Filberts, brights, and flats bound with soft camel hair. And while he has a light taste for libertarianism, he doesn't ask me to do outdoor activities, so it kind of squares. We spend weekends in bed, moving quickly out of the first nervous touches into the realm where we are undeterred by the odd turns of the id. But of course, my failure is hanging between us. He is infinitely more talented in the thing I most want to do, and he seems to prefer it that way. It is silly how late this occurs to me, the carrots he dangles in his boredom, how casually he reaches for the stick. I see myself in the women who trail him, the moony typographers, the perky-breasted RISD grads. Still, eventually I go over to his house and beg him to look at my work. I get on my knees, offer up my sketchbook, and say goodbye to his apartment and the sinewy watercolors he sometimes shows me at 3:00 a.m.

There is a painting that I love by Artemisia Gentileschi, *Judith Slaying Holofernes*. In it, two women are decapitating a man. They hold him down as he struggles to push away the blade. It is a brutal, tenebrist masterpiece, drenched in carotid blood. Gentileschi painted it after her mentor, Agostino Tassi, was convicted of her rape. As I am working on a piece inspired by this painting, my father dies. I bury him next to my mother, and for weeks I don't sleep and the mice eat all my fruit. Mark sends his condolences in a card, but then he stops returning my calls. He sends the drawings I left at his house in an envelope simply labelled *stuff*, and I leave him some voicemails that mostly boil down to him being a hack who only draws four-fingered hands, to how he is an impossible dweeb who needs to be kept away from women and shot into space, and a few times, yes, I stand in front of his house in the middle of the night. I draft some emails I don't send and wander the halls of the office with all the things I want to say to his face. But when I see him now, when I go back into the stairwell next to Kevin's office and see how Mark has remained unchanged, how he is flanked by two women and proceeding gaily about his life, I lose my nerve.

That night I meet Eric at a wine bar in the Village, and the man I find waiting in the back of the bar does not seem to be the man I met two days before. He is wearing the same skin, but more tightly, as if something immaterial and supermassive spit him out at the mouth of the bar and he is just going with it, waiting for me to call his bluff.

"You're late," he says after he orders a glass of Côtes du Rhône for himself and a gin and tonic for me. His tone is so cold, I can't tell if he wants an explanation, or if this stern incarnation of him is a joke. He looks different, even older now, his suit jacket slung around the back of his chair. By contrast, the dress I'm wearing is 80 percent spandex.

"Sorry."

"I just like to be on time."

"There was train traffic," I say, and he laughs.

"I don't miss those days."

"You don't take the train?"

"No, I don't," he says, and I like him less and more. Less because he appears now to be soft and impractical, and more because this is something he can afford to be. "You look good," he says, making a show of taking me in, and it feels good to be consumed like this, to have decorated myself specifically for him, and for him to sit on the other side of the table and unravel all the crepe.

"So do you. How was work?"

"I don't want to talk about work. Do you want to talk about work?"

"I mean, I guess not."

"Where is that wine?" he asks, and then a waitress is leaning between us to pour a thimbleful of wine into his glass, which he circles and then sucks impatiently through his teeth.

"Fine," he says, watching closely as she pours the rest. He waves her away and takes a long, indulgent drink. "I'm a little nervous, so I'm sorry if I seem—" He takes another drink, directs all his attention to the middle of my face.

"It's all right," I say, but it comes out a little patronizing. He gives me a hard look and finishes his drink, which is something of a feat, as it was a very generous pour. The waitress comes back around and looks at Eric with big, admiring eyes. "Can I have a little more?" I ask when I see that my gin and tonic is mostly ice.

"Good idea," Eric says, and we start in earnest on a few G&Ts. It gets us loose enough to talk about politics, but as he talks, I hold my breath. I know we are in agreement on the most general, least controversial ideological points—women are people, racism is bad, Florida will be underwater in fifty years—but there is still ample time for him to bring up how much he enjoyed *Atlas Shrugged*. Even with good men, you are always waiting for the surprise. I ask for another drink and he pauses and laughs.

"Do you maybe want to talk about something else?"

"Why?"

"You seem a little tense," he says, reaching under the table to touch my knee.

"Have you noticed how the waitress is looking at you?"

"Not really," he says, and slides his hand under my dress. Our table is not particularly private, but I don't want him to stop. I take another drink as he rests the back of his hand on the inside of my thigh. "So we have arrived at the second date."

"Yes."

"And you want to keep doing this?"

"Yes," I say, even though I don't quite know what he means.

"I'd like to lay my cards on the table," he says, withdrawing his hand. "My life is established. I have been married to the same woman for thirteen years and our graves are right next to each other."

"Sure." It occurs to me that we are now having a serious conversation, but I have not even had a moment to pull my dress back down. He pulls out a piece of paper and flattens it out with his hand.

"And so to introduce something new into my life, into this whole"—he glances at the paper—"marital framework, there have to be boundaries."

"Of course."

"And those boundaries have to be established early. Because"—he grabs my hand, which feels like something he has practiced—"I think we should keep doing this. What do you think?" I think that thirteen years off the market has made him vulnerable in a way that feels unethical to exploit. And yet.

"Yes, definitely."

"So, the rules," he says, looking down at the paper. I steal a look, slide it out from under his hand, and this is the first time I make contact with his wife.

"Your wife wrote this," I say, scanning what seem to be bullet points before what seem to be words. The paper is soft and deeply creased, as if it has been folded and unfolded frequently.

"She has terrible handwriting, doesn't she?" he says, and when I lower the paper and look at him, I see him, the man who took me to the park. He smiles, this small cruelty hanging in the air between us. And though I can tell he feels a little bad about having said it, he seems relieved when I join in.

"It doesn't even look like English," I say, and here is a brief account of the month we spent adhering to the rules: First, to my great disappointment, the second date does not yield any sex. I starve through the whole night on gin and little bits of bread, and we stumble through the dark and fool around in the park. The fact of us both being shadows facilitates a compulsive honesty between us, and I tell him that during the weekends, sometimes I lie in one spot and don't move until I have to go to the bathroom or to work, and he tells me that he is sterile, and we laugh because rule number one is that we cannot have unprotected sex. But after we laugh, he is sunken in the middle, withdrawn in a way that is cemented by drink, and we watch a bride float through Washington Square at midnight, the tulle and taffeta blue in the gauzy light, and I think about his wife and wonder if she is right-handed, if she is self-conscious about her handwriting or beautiful enough that she doesn't have to be.

And when Eric turns to look at me, whatever connective tissue is responsible for securing his eyeballs has been boozed to a mere suggestion, and because of the wind I can sort of see where he is beginning to lose his hair, and someone across the way is playing "Mary Had a Little Lamb" on the guitar in a minor key when he seems to find one complete moment of sobriety and focus this violence on my mouth, which fits into his unevenly in a way that makes our kiss asynchronous and wet, even as we are chapped from all the gin.

On the third date, I am sure we are going to have sex. I shave everywhere, take a straight razor to my arms and legs, hold the blade at thirty degrees as a brownout courses through my neighborhood, and when I arrive at the clinic, he kisses my neck and whispers in my ear and we both get tested for STDs. The fluorescents wash him out, but on this occasion his neurosis is full bleed, and he tells me he does not like hospitals, because they smell like urine and synthetic gardenias, and also he is terrified of dying, and theoretically so am I, but theoretically, what if I'm not, though saying this out loud is ungenerous, and so I tell him, yes, living is definitely what I want to keep on doing, it has been great so far. But mostly I'm hoping I don't have chlamydia, and so I miss a great deal of what he tells me about his fear of death, and I notice a pamphlet with a white baby on it, and after our tests come back clean and we go for burgers, I don't eat anything because I still want to have sex, but I'm still thinking about the baby, about the potential softness of its head, and as I'm thinking about this abortion I had at sixteen, his wife calls him and he leaves, because it is July 3, barbeque prep needs to be done, and one of the rules is that if she calls, he has to go. During this exchange he has over the phone, a tendril of her voice peals through the air, wireless and sweet, and he says, *Rebecca, come on, Rebecca.* And between dates four and six I am feverishly looking her up, but Rebecca Walker is too common a name and Eric, while committed to the digitization of flaked glass plate negatives in his professional life, refuses to submit to the inevitability of the digitization of his own thoughts, meals, and whereabouts out of self-righteous Luddism or general oldness, meaning I cannot find her through him, and I lie awake at night and ponder the Twitters of a dozen generic white women, looking for clues and only finding interchangeable results. By date seven there is still no sex, which is getting insulting, but I will debase myself entirely to get the things that I want and so on all the way through our ninth date, after we have been seeing each other in person for a month, I am doing what I will with Popsicles and bananas and yanking him into the bathroom by his lapels, this close to threatening him, and he laughs at me and tells me softly, *stop*, because he is a little old-fashioned and finds my behavior embarrassing, and because my embarrassment typically inverts into anger, I shove him away and am surprised and pleased when he shoves me back. His contrition is immediate and effusive, but I have already archived the look on his face, the glimmer of teeth, the glee with which he exercises his strength. And when he helps me up from the ground the heft in his hand is the contact that will sustain me for five days because one of the rules is that his wife can change the rules and one of the new rules is that we can only see each other on the

weekends. And so, regrettably, on Sunday he is climbing the
stairs to my apartment because it is the only private place I know
where I might coerce him out of his clothes. The salmon smell
is gone, but my roommate is on the couch clipping her toenails
in her terrifying vitamin C sheet mask and up until this point I
have sufficiently hidden the extent of my poverty. But now he is
going to see the puckered linoleum and the casserole dishes collecting water in our bathroom. He's going to know that he hasn't
been taking me out to restaurants so much as providing much-
needed calories, and when he comes up the stairs, his face is
shiny and incredulous, like what has happened to him is terrible
but he is impressed enough by the novelty to persevere. He
closes the door behind him, and my roommate is raising her
eyebrows behind her mask, because not even in my own home
am I safe from this look, this acknowledgment of our asymmetry, which even in New York is a stumbling block for waitresses
and cabbies and which Eric is totally oblivious to, even as I am
routinely making assurances that yes, we are going to the same
place, and yes, it is a single check. Because you have to go
through the bathroom to get to the kitchen, and through the
kitchen to get to my bedroom, he basically gets a complete tour
and is so kind about the whole thing he doesn't even mention
the Rice-A-Roni my roommate has left on the back of the toilet.
In fact, as I lock the bedroom door behind me, he seems to find
the whole thing very adventurous, though when he thinks I'm
not looking I can tell he is concerned. I can tell he is revising me
in his head, trying to square the concept of my adulthood with
the sixth-floor walk-up and the parameters of my room, which
allow for only a futon and a poster of MF Doom. As I am

standing with my back to the door and he settles down on my futon, gingerly, like he's afraid the frame will not support his weight, I know that the dissonance is finally dawning on him in a serious way. And while I never enter a room without wondering what personal adjustments need to be made, it is strange to see something similar happen to this friendly, white, midwestern man. It is strange to see him noticing about himself what I always notice—the optimism, the presumption, this rarefied alternate reality in which there is nowhere he does not belong. He looks around with this gentle horror in his eyes, as if it has just occurred to him—upon the introduction of this economic dimension—the mutual desperation involved in merging two people at opposite ends of life. And then he spots my paint and a blank canvas and I run over to close the closet door but it is too late. He wants to know why I've never mentioned it and if I'm any good. And I don't know if it's because the whole night has been humiliating, but I tell him yes, I'm pretty good, which is another mistake because of course he wants me to commit him to paint. So I pull some Stoli from underneath my bed and pour it into the one clean mug I have and we take turns drinking from it, wilting in the heat and forgiving the gulf between us long enough to halfway undress, and he is not a great model, slouching and always changing the direction of his head, but as he reclines, half out of his clothes with his long arms and faint freckles and chaos of curly graying hair, I remember my body and become sensitive to his, to the dwindling proportion of air in the room, to the way he looks at me as I establish my palette, like he isn't just humoring me. Like he is taking me seriously. And while I appreciate his seriousness, it makes me sick to my stomach. It spoils his beauty into a series of halftones between creases of flesh. The lilac and bice blue, the potency of a little titanium white, and the vodka fattening his tongue when he says he's sorry he pushed me, and I say how sorry are you and he says very sorry and I say then beg for my forgiveness, which he does adequately while I give him head, finally, for the first time, my bedroom deadly silent except for his soft, breathless apologies, which I think he actually means as he carefully moves my hair out of the way, though later I clean the acrylic from his thighs and tell him actually, I'd like it if he pushed me again. He thinks I'm joking, and when he realizes I'm not, his face darkens and he says he doesn't feel comfortable with that. This is the last time he comes to my apartment. When we go out to eat a few days later, I see that he is aware that he is feeding me, as much as I'm aware that there is a large part of his life I cannot see, a place in Jersey with a driveway and a mailbox and extra towels, sustained on imagination alone because one of the rules is that I am not allowed inside his house. And things come up. One of us gets sick, I can't muster enough will to open my mail or wash my hair, he has a business trip or a dinner party with Rebecca, and by the time we meet again, we have forgotten how we fit. We are in a state of constant regression, distance rendering the details too slippery to grasp. And then on a Thursday night, day fifty-two of our excruciatingly chaste courtship, he calls me and tells me to meet him at this club in SoHo and to wear something short.

I do what he says, even though I have given up on the prospect of sex, because it turns out maybe he is the only friend I have. So I eat half a chocolate cake and arrive at the club in cutoffs and sneakers, so ready to fuck that when someone brushes up against me on the train I make a scary, involuntary noise. Eric emerges from the club through a wall of smoke and pulls me inside with his large, clammy hand, and all around me are the campy trappings of 1975. He leads me to the center of the pit by the tips of my fingers and the air is thick with mist and sweat and plumes of artificial fog, the strobe and smoke machine's combined effort churning out these puffy, orange convex knives and I sneeze into my elbow and make eye contact with a dog who is sitting in the corner chewing someone's silk slipper, which bums me out, as it always does when animals look to be in places they don't want to be. A parade of synthetic fabrics move in unison under the liquid clip of light like a school of silver herring as some bunting near the stage that says *Fever!* pulls away from the ceiling and it occurs to me that this is one of those places in the business of reproducing a decade for a night because the bulletin by the door indicates that in a few weeks it will be the nineties. But for now a workable hologram of Chaka Khan overtakes Gloria Gaynor and her bouncy curls and Chaka is cooing in her famed shredded panties, squatting and saluting at the end of the stage, flexing her brown thighs and smirking into the crowd, though the music that is actually playing is KC and the Sunshine Band's "That's the Way," which makes it feel a little spectral, which is how nights like these always feel once the strobes lift for a moment and you see the beer and glitter on the floor, the reanimation of what is dead repackaged and called nostalgia and all that earnest time travel tempered with irony because as I look around almost everyone is dancing but with the sort of shrugging participation that conveys this whole thing as joke, like, how lame, like, I dig this, but not too much. But the beauty of disco is the too much, is the horn section and the cheese, and so Eric and I convene in the bathroom over a spoon and someone is in the stall next to us with bare feet weeping and we go out into the middle and Eric is a very coordinated white man but given to fall back on the cabbage patch and the diddy bop, which is fine, and then we're in his car with the AC all the way up, on a reasonable clip through the Holland Tunnel, and he's handing me his phone and asking me to decline a call from his wife, which makes me feel terrible, not out of any fealty to Rebecca but because this night appears to have generated from some greater marital drama, though of course I relish denying the call, just as I relish the wave of cicadas rippling the air as we pull up to his house, which does indeed have a mailbox with a flag and *Walker* on the side in a jaunty yellow font, and up the stairs and inside his bedroom all the pictures are facedown, which is a level of premeditation that gives me pause, but that ultimately eases me out of my clothes because to do all this he would have to know I would say yes, he would have to believe himself capable of finessing the initial yes into the terminal yes in such perfect order that I would even go to Jersey and the idea that he understands this, his total control of the situation, is what does me in. There is no foreplay. I am still in my socks trying to discern from the wallpaper a conclusion about the marriage that results in this, this man peeling off his *Disco Sucks* shirt and pulling me into his lap and apologizing about the delay because it has been thirteen years with the same woman, he says, thirteen years, and all the rules have changed, and so I try to help him out of his pants but his shoes are still on, shoes with laces that we both consider for a moment before we opt out and get his pants down only as far as they need to go, his face dark and urgent, his body taut and smattered with coarse, curly hair. Slowly, he eases me down onto his grand, slightly left-leaning cock, and for a moment I do rethink my atheism, for a moment I consider the possibility of God as a chaotic, amorphous evil who made autoimmune disease but gave us miraculous genitals to cope, and so I fuck him desperately with the force of this epiphany and Eric is talkative and filthy but there is some derangement about his face, this pink contortion that introduces the whites of his eyes in a way that makes me afraid he might say something we cannot recover from just yet, so I cover his mouth and say shut up, shut the fuck up, which is more aggressive than I would normally be at this point but it gets the job done and in general if you need a pick-me-up I welcome you to make a white man your bitch though I feel panicked all of a sudden to have not used a condom and I'm looking around the room and there is a bathroom attached, and in the bathroom are what look to be extra towels and that makes me so emotional that he pauses and in one instant a concerned host rises out of his violent sexual mania, slowing the proceedings into the dangerous territory of eye contact and lips and tongue where mistakes get made and you forget that everything eventually dies, so it is not my fault that during this juncture I call him daddy and it is definitely not my fault that this gets him off so swiftly that he says he loves me and we are collapsing back in satiation and horror, not speaking until he gets me a car home and says take care of yourself like, please go, and as the car is pulling away he is standing there on the porch in a floral silk robe that is clearly his wife's, looking like he has not so much had an orgasm as experienced an arduous exorcism, and a cat is sitting at his feet, utterly bemused by the white clapboard and verdant lawn, which makes me hate this cat as the city rises around me in a bouquet of dust, industrial soot, and overripe squash, insisting upon its own enormity like some big-dick postmodernist fiction and still beautiful despite its knowledge of itself, even as the last merciless days of July leave large swaths of the city wilted and blank.

And then for a week Eric doesn't answer my texts, or my emails, or my calls, and I am maintaining my smile in the middle of my open office plan, leafing through this new book we're putting out on the virtues of sharing. And now I know where he lives so ten days after having fucked him in the bed he shares with his wife I go right up to the door and find it unlocked, and no one is home, so I walk around the house and pick up these cold lemons on the counter and roll them around in my hands, and I open the fridge and take a drink of milk and carry the carton up to the bedroom where a door opens to a closet with a collection of women's clothes and I gather the silk and wool and cashmere in my hands and then there is a voice, and I turn and standing in the doorway of the attached bathroom in yellow rubber gloves and a T-shirt that says *Yale* is his wife.

3

got the abortion in my junior year of high school. There was a brief moment when I considered the pregnancy, when I tried to halve a grain of sand and accommodate its ambition to yield a pair of lungs. At the time, I worked retail at a dying mall. Eighteen hours a week smoothing chinos and shadowing aggressive Quebecois customers who came to upstate New York to exploit our low-priced bids to stay in business. There were only four stores open in the mall. A CVS that kept the animal crackers next to the douches, a Deb with five-dollar packs of high-waisted panties, a gun shop, and my store, a scrappy little boutique for the professional woman. I was a miserable sales associate, prone to confessional spirals during my attempts to move the store loyalty card, but an asset as long as I did enough work to afford the veteran associates more time to socialize. During lunchtime, I manned the store alone, and the two other associates suspended their concerns about my awkwardness with customers to go have lunch at Boston Market. That I was not invited to these lunches felt more like a kindness than a slight. They were good to me, inclined to bring back some creamed spinach and runny macaroni, which I ate by a defunct Key Bank whose ATMs were filled with honeycomb. During this time, I couldn't tell if I liked being alone, or if I only endured it because I knew I had no choice.

I was not popular and I was not unpopular. To invite admiration or ridicule, you first have to be seen. So the story of the cell that once divided inside me and its subsequent obliteration is also the story of the first man who saw me. The man who owned the gun shop, Clay, a metalhead who was pathological in the maintenance of his teeth. He was the seventh black person I'd met in Latham. Mixed-race, a riotous Punnett square of dominant Korean and Nigerian genes, so ethnically ambiguous that under different kinds of light he appeared to be different men. The first day we met, he was smoking a cigarette on the DDR machine outside the shuttered movie theater. He told me that he was in debt and that he and his brother were no longer speaking and there was something so easy about his immediate familiarity that I told him how my mother died. How I found her with one shoe still on. How I kept painting this moment and found no format suitable. How it had only been five months since her death and my father was already seeing someone. This was the contradiction that would define me for years, my attempt to secure undiluted solitude and my swift betrayal of this effort once in the spotlight of an interested man. I was pretending not to worry about the consequences of my isolation. But whenever I talked to anyone, I found myself overcompensating for the atrophy of my social muscles.

I was happy to be included in something, even if it was a mostly one-sided conversation with a man twice my age. We met on my lunch breaks and he bought me ice cream. I sat in his station wagon and watched him load and unload his gun. I leaned over the display case with the tanto-point knives and let him run his fingers through my hair. When he asked me how old I was, I lied. When I told him my father had not been home for weeks, he made sure I had money for food, and sometimes he would call and make me tell him what I had to eat. But still there were moments I felt his caution, a surprising squareness about his use of profanity, unsubtle inquiries about the ages of the imaginary boyfriends I supplied.

On our fifth lunch date, he plucked a caping knife from the display and pressed it into my hands, the shop's familiar rotation of Swedish death metal a murmur against the weight of the oak and steel. Even as he tried to preserve the part of me that was apparently untouched, sometimes I felt he was trying to scare me. As kids are, I was especially responsive to this challenge, determined to be stoic and game. So we got Red Bulls at the CVS, and he pierced my ears using a Zippo and a self-threading needle. We drove to his house, a squat double-wide in Troy, and he made me steak and showed me his antique guns. There was something automated about him, an offhanded perpetual motion, the inevitability of a weapon in his hands and the unconscious priming of the weapon to do what it was made to do, his attention elsewhere as he seated rounds in the magazine and tugged the slide. The way he would talk without prompting or encouragement, as if all this time, he had been waiting, desperately, for a captive audience. But there were moments that neutralized my fear, moments he passed the store as I was firming up the sale rack, and in the air was a mutual understanding that we were both looking for something to destroy, that we were people of color in a town that was colorless, a language developing between us that wasn't so much romantic as it was breathless with shared conspiracy. So when he pressed the caping knife into my hand, I took this to mean that to him, I had become a person. He had considered me and noted my deliberation, my central nervous system, the possibility that even within my small, teenage universe, I might have a reason to kill.

At home, I pressed the cold, flat side of the knife against my thigh. I watched thirty-eight minutes of porn on the family computer, and then I took a bus to Clay's house. He didn't ask any questions. He only opened the door and pulled me inside. It happened in the dark. I followed him into his bedroom, and everything smelled like cordite and ash. His body was heavy and he trembled when he came. I felt my power in the high, desperate sound of his pleasure. I felt my error in how little I thought it would mean. I didn't tell him I was a virgin because I could not bear to be treated tenderly. I didn't want him to be careful. I wanted it to be over with. So when it hurt and I was too proud to say *stop* and so said *more*, I believed, like a Catholic or a Tortured Artist, that the merit of a commitment correlates directly to the pain you endure in its pursuit. I left his house and bled privately at home, happy to have done the thing that everyone is supposed to do. I had thought it would feel better, but I was new. Initiated and lean, like I had been shorn of all my hair and let into a bright, secret room. Each time we fucked, there were fewer words, moments a sudden and inscrutable darkness would find its way into the room as he pressed me down. *I'm not a bad person*, he said, as I put on my shoes. And then I was pregnant. Then my father came home, the car smashed in on one side. I didn't ask him where he'd been and he didn't ask who knocked me up. When I told him, I said that it was someone from school. Without comment, he drove me to the clinic, and when it was over, he drove me back home. He brought me tea and ibuprofen, and then left the house for another week. During that week, there was more blood than reasonable. There was the vague feeling I had escaped something preposterous. And there was my mother's record collection. I hadn't gone into my mother's room for months, but I unearthed Donna Summer's *Four Seasons of Love* and hooked it onto the player. I opened the windows and let some air in, and a laugh bloomed and promptly died behind my teeth. A moment in which a joyless and reflexive action of the throat gave me hope that at some point, another laugh might follow.

When I turn and see Eric's wife, a current passes through an open window and it is the perfect iteration of that stale spring— the dust and vinyl, the interior of Clay's station wagon powdered in ash, my underwear bloodied at the bottom of the trash—and there is a sound in the room, a scream I recognize as my own laughter.

My laugh, the real one, is a robust, ugly thing that has, on occasion, startled the drink right out of a date's hands. So full credit is due when there is only the barest inclination on her face that she has heard it. I stand there with the sleeve of her silk blouse crushed in my fist and I think how strange it would be to say her name, to acknowledge that I know who she is even as she and Eric have taken such care to arrange our separation. It seems impossible that this amorphous Essex County specter with no distinct social media presence is standing before me, and that her name is Rebecca.

I try to reconcile the woman I have imagined with the woman before me, but there is too much data, and too many of my assumptions have quietly become absolutes. I make amendments reluctantly, surprised by the beauty of her feet. Otherwise she is exceedingly regular, everything about her so nondescript as to almost be sinister, the halo of dirty-blond hair around her sun-battered face, her boyish lean, the invisible segue of thigh into calf, and the general feeling that if she took her clothes off, her body would be as smooth and as featureless as silt.

I turn away from the closet to face her as she peels off her gloves. There is a moment when I think she is preparing to punch me. She moves toward me, her carriage so upright it would be funny if it weren't so eerie in its apparent deliberation. And it's not that I'm scared, but the idea of forming complete sentences and listening to her complete sentences in this room with an unmade bed I have once assisted in unmaking seems unbearable, and so I turn and run down the stairs, and I look over my shoulder and see that she is coming after me, her hair catching a shaft of sun, the indignity of what we're doing turning my stomach as I cut through the kitchen and into the backyard, where she falls through a sprinkler, her feet losing their tread on the grass.

Technically I am home free, but then I turn and see the turf on her knees. I see a neighbor kid watching from his aboveground pool, and I am embarrassed, shamed by the lazy tenor of the cul-de-sac. The gardenias and unsecured bicycles and me, breathing heavily over someone's wife. So I walk back and take her damp hands into mine, then pull her to her feet.

"I know who you are but I don't want to discuss it, if that's all right with you," she says, dusting herself off. "I just wasn't finished looking at you. I didn't expect you to be so young. It's awful."

"Awful?"

"Yes, for you," she says, and the neighbor kid slips out of the pool and runs back into his house.

"It's late. You should stay for dinner," she says, thumbing a bruise that is forming on her arm, and it is an understatement to say that I would rather do anything else, but then I feel her expectation, that she is not so much asking a question as allowing me time to confirm an obvious conclusion—that in exchange for her compromise, for her coolness about what has just happened, something is owed. She directs me to a guest room with its own bathroom, looks me over, and says, *Humid, isn't it*, which is an indirect way of bringing my attention to a thing I am already aware of—this glandular free-for-all happening underneath my clothes. I look in the mirror, and my face is shining. She shows me the towels and suggests that I wash up. When I emerge from the shower, a dress is laid out on the bed, cornflower blue and immediately recognizable to me as something I would likely never be able to afford, a totem of a realm where sticker price is incidental data, a realm so theoretical that when I consider what I would have to do to enter it, I can only think of my debt, an aggrieved Sallie Mae representative standing above me while I sleep.

As I try to put on the dress, it is the first time I suspect she is trying to humiliate me. It is so small that squeezing into it comes at the expense of 90 percent of my mobility. This potential cruelty is so specific, so much like a courtesy that has merely gone awry, that I feel obligated to be a good sport. I consider leaving through the window, but then I see there are cars gathered outside, a steady stream of guests funneling into the house. Standing within this wave of guests is Eric, home from work, greeting everyone at the door. He checks his watch and frowns. It is 7:00 p.m., and apparently this is when adult parties start. I remind myself that I wanted to demonstrate my seriousness, to show him that I will not be ignored, even as I consider the reality of confronting him and panic. Seeing him through the window, though, I find his aggressive normalcy insulting. I think: *I can be normal, too.*

So I hobble down the stairs, every degree of motion a threat to the integrity of the single zipper separating my breasts from everyone in the room. I wish I had known there would be this many people, and Rebecca's omission of this information makes me wonder if she is, in fact, fucking with me. It's clear she is a magician of some sort: in the short time it has taken me to shower and dress, the place has been transformed into a heavily creped exercise in adult merriment, the confetti and clusters of graphic foil balloons a disorienting mixture against the faint thrum of monk-heavy New Age. But the woman of the house is nowhere to be found.

I brace myself to be seen by him, prepare to appear incidental and cool, but still I search the crowd for the white of an eye. I seize the details, the deliberate—the fruity dental office artwork, the shelves of crystal, the unsmiling shot of Eric and Rebecca in the ruins of Pompeii—and everything fermenting underneath, the sagging garbage in the kitchen, a still-moist handprint on the TV. I take a crab cake from a server just for something to do with my hands. I want to eat it and give my stomach something more to do than churn around the bile steadily rising into my mouth, but otherwise I feel beyond food, beyond the vulnerabilities of my intestinal tract, and this is so unprecedented that it doesn't even bother me that every available beverage appears to be nonalcoholic.

The guest who is standing beside me seems to come to the same realization, his face souring as he palms a Sprite. He turns and I feel him assessing me, trying to figure out how I fit, the makeup of the party so homogeneous it gives me up as a matter of course. Normally I would be unconcerned about this level of scrutiny, but I am completely sober, the dress hindering my ability to breathe.

"How do you know the couple?" he asks, and then something catches my eye across the room. A black child in a pink wig and a tummy shirt, smoking a candy cigarette.

"Who is that?"

"Because I've never seen you before."

"What?" I say, scanning his muppety body for any sign of definition before I turn and see that the girl is gone.

"You didn't go to Yale, did you?" he asks, and the phrasing of this question doesn't escape my notice. I can't say why I have always felt obligated to impress even men I don't want to fuck, but I'm embarrassed by the prospect of his pity, this man I don't know and will likely never see again. So I don't say I dropped out of art school after sending some incoherent Comic Sans poems to the department chair. I don't say I enrolled in an indistinct community college, threw away most of my paintings, and graduated with what is arguably a more useless degree.

"I work with Rebecca," I say, which, out of all the available lies, is the one I can support the least. I think I see Eric on the other side of the room but it is just a lamp.

"So you raise the dead."

"What?"

"I guess someone has to do the dirty work, right?"

"Yes, I guess."

"I can't believe they made it fourteen years."

"Who?"

"Rebecca and Eric?" He points above me, and when I look, I see there is a detail I missed. A banner that reads: *The Lace Anniversary.* "Kind of a weird one to celebrate. Though I guess it is a feat. Do you ever look at them when they're together? Like different species," he says, and we look at each other as I catch up to the conversation we are really having. A conversation that always happens on the fringes of someone else's good fortune— the murmurs of disbelief, envy. It puts me at ease. I smile at him and move into the crowd.

I am not good at parties. The music, either a squeaky-clean parade of *Now That's What I Call Music,* or curated by someone who thinks they discovered Portishead, everyone waiting for the segue into late-night power balladry or self-conscious karaoke, looking around to gauge the right amount of participation, "Don't Stop Believin'" or "Push It" underneath the inevitability of a regular colonoscopy. The too close and too wet—the shout

I receive into my face, a stranger's spit underneath my eyelid, in my drink, the wine spilling between my fingers as I try to escape the person at the party who is especially desperate not to be caught standing alone. It is a foregone conclusion I will once or twice hurt someone's feelings deeply because of something I say or a face I make, which I will of course think about when I ride the train home, and actually, forever, even though I tried to be merry and keep the conversation light, even though I can't sleep and I can't shit, and someone is dying but that one song tells you to slide to the left and you have no choice.

I stand on the fringe of these starched, professional circles and try to follow the narrative arc of a stranger's portfolio. And then as someone is deep into an account of a deck renovation and simultaneously a screed about the sympathy we should all have for the police, the child in the pink wig is climbing the stairs, her brown Kewpie face opening when she turns and looks directly into my eyes. The moment it happens, it's clear the eye contact is a mistake, that she'd glanced at the crowd and did not mean to find me looking. But the surprise on her face is short-lived as she cools, turns away, and continues up the stairs. Then Rebecca appears, practically out of thin air.

"I could use your help," she says, pulling me across the room and into the kitchen. Once inside, I swat her away and try to regain some dignity.

"Happy anniversary," I say as she shakes the drawer, reaches inside.

"Thanks," she says, arching an eyebrow at her watch. I take

her in. She is, I suppose, sexy in the way a triangle can be sexy, the clean pivot from point A to B to C, her body and face breaking no rules, following each other in a way that is logical and curt. Of course, in motion, when she turns and stoops to open the oven, the geometry is weirder. She takes the cake out and kicks the door closed. She opens a tub of frosting, pops the tabs on the cake tin, and takes a generous dollop of frosting onto the spatula.

"Is my husband drinking?"

"What?" I ask, watching as she tries to frost the cake, which is still too hot to take the spread.

"Does Eric drink when he's with you?"

"No," I lie, adjusting my breasts. I put a palm to my forehead and find that it is slick.

"He shouldn't be drinking."

"Why?" I say, wiping my palms on the dress, only to find that the fabric, this slippery second skin, does not absorb the moisture. Rebecca looks up at me through her hair, a bead of sweat pearling at her hairline, rolling down onto one false, mink lash. As Rebecca reaches into a bag of confectioner's sugar with her bare hand, I think of Eric's flushed face, the time he pushed me to the floor. How I wanted him to do it again.

"I know you've been here before." She stacks one layer on top of the other, filling oozing down the sides. She looks at me directly, and this is the first time I notice her eyes are gray.

"You were in our bedroom," she says. "I could feel it. Everything was so neat." She puts her hand on my shoulder. "I know you don't understand. I can tell you've never owned anything," she says, and then she withdraws and says it's time to bring out the cake. When I look at it, it is perhaps the least appetizing thing I have ever seen. She puts the cake onto a platter and carries it out to the party. As I follow her out, I notice that there is a door by the pantry, and beyond this door a dark side street, haloed in lamplight and slick with rain. She is halfway into the other room, something exhausted between us that makes me certain it wouldn't matter if I left. I can't say why I don't.

And there he is, standing in the center of the room, the lights dimming as Rebecca gives him the platter. He holds it awkwardly, frowns as a camera flash blooms from the back of the room and throws the moment into sharp relief. Rebecca pulls a candle from behind her ear, asks the room for a light. When one is supplied, she turns to me and places it in my hand. Amid his effort to balance the cake, Eric notices me. What happens to him then, a sudden and swiftly contained conniption that draws all the color from his face, is not half as delicious as it should be. Eric's fly is down and this current iteration, this soft, breathing haircut—I can't say what it is, but I get this feeling that this is actually his most honest form, and it really pisses me off.

So I light the candle and recede into the dark as another flash tears through the room and Rebecca starts singing into a mic with a cord that a guest coming from the bathroom nearly trips over, her hair platinum in the flash when it becomes apparent to everyone in the room that Rebecca hasn't opted for a standard lovey-dovey Beach Boys or Boyz II Men but a Phil Collins joint, arguably *the* Phil Collins joint, with no musical accompaniment, the negative space of the original song having nothing on this rendition, this staggered delivery that makes clear to everyone in the room that she is taking no artistic liberties and remaining faithful to the song's true pacing, which in a silent room makes it sort of an ordeal, creates a desperation on the part of the crowd that after each curt pause, her voice be able to take these familiar turns. Her voice is mostly amelodic, and between the choice of song and the cramped space of the living room, everyone is attuned to her copious lyrical mistakes. It is unclear if she is singing to anyone in particular, though Eric is doing his best to be a good audience, smiling wearily for whichever lovers of chaos are still taking photos with the flash. The cake nearly slides off the platter when he turns to look at me, and I turn to look at Rebecca, who is, despite everything, the most comfortable person in the room. She raises her arm above her head on the segue into *it's no stranger to you and me*, and as one is wont to do after this verse, the whole room is braced for the breakdown, which Rebecca accommodates with a pause so sustained that I hear someone across the street scream, *Where is the dog!* before Rebecca ties up her cover, brings the lights back up, and starts clapping for herself, which we all dutifully echo back.

All this time Eric hasn't looked away from me, within his confusion a promise of retribution that I find thrilling—historically the sort of high sweetest at its inception, when a man's wrath is just a consideration, when he curtails the impulse because he thinks he's different while you know he is the same. As Rebecca takes a handful of cake and forces it into his mouth, the room fills with laughter and I turn and climb the stairs, partly to go to the bathroom and partly to be alone. I look through their cabinets and find it a surprisingly unsatisfying activity, not just because everything is generic and OTC, but because I have come to the part of the night where I am incapable of any uppercase emotion, and every circuit responsible for my cellular regeneration has begun to smoke.

This is the conclusion to most parties I attend, and it usually helps to take a moment alone in the bathroom, though the inevitable presence of a mirror can complicate things. Even if I have done the adequate mental jujitsu to convince myself that I appear like a normal human being, a trip to the bathroom to regroup can on occasion turn into the kind of fun-house voodoo that happens in DMV photos and long exposures of Victorian children. There is something about looking into someone else's mirror, something that always gives me more information than I need. In the past three years I have tried to turn lemons into lemonade by reciting old Tumblr affirmations into these mirrors, but it hasn't helped.

I take some cough syrup out of the cabinet and take a long drink. I look in the mirror and I do not hate how I look, nor have I ever, even though I am not usually the prettiest person in the room. My biggest issue when I look into the mirror is that sometimes the face I see doesn't feel like mine.

"I am happy to be alive. I am happy to be alive."

"What are you doing?" a voice says, and I turn around and find the kid in the wig eating a slice of pizza.

"You're real."

"Obviously," she says. There are times I interact with kids and recall my abortion fondly, moments like this when I cross paths with a child who is clearly a drag.

"Obviously," I say, screwing the cap back on the cough syrup.

"I've never seen you before."

"Probably because we don't run in the same circles, kid."

"There are no black people in this neighborhood," she says, and I catch my reflection in the mirror and feel a tightness in my chest.

"What's your name?"

"Akila."

"Are there really no black people in this neighborhood?" I ask, just as Eric appears behind her.

"Go to your room, please," he says, and Akila shrugs and disappears down the hall. He waits for her door to close and then closes the space between us, and when I look up at him I receive him anew. His overwhelming height, the intensity of his eye contact, the general feeling that he is not a man who sleeps. To some extent I've had to revise him every time we've met, but this feels different. The last time I saw him was the first time I ever saw him come, an elastic split second made for paint, somehow analogous to the expression he is making as he tries to find the words, his mouth opening and closing without sound. I like this part. I remind myself of this when I realize I am nervous, when I notice how incongruously this degree of anger hangs on him, and that I cannot anticipate how this anger will manifest.

"What are you doing in my house?"

"Congratulations on the anniversary."

"What is the matter with you?"

"Everything is the matter," I say, just as Rebecca appears. She pauses and looks at us.

"I was thinking we could start a game of Trivial Pursuit," she says, and now that I look between them and consider them as a unit, they do seem like different species: Rebecca a lonely, carnivorous bird, Eric a vegetarian mammal with a short, panicked life.

"I'm going to take her home," he says.

"This is our anniversary party."

"Yes, I know." He fishes his keys out of his pocket, grabs my arm, and starts ushering me down the stairs.

"Okay, so call a car," Rebecca says.

"The capital of Kansas is Topeka. Rosebud was the sled," he says before he pulls me down the stairs and out of the door, then stuffs me into the car. Nothing about the interior of the car has changed. It is still vaguely moist, still smacking of something lightly fried, still old in a way that has less to do with the window cranks than the whine of the steering wheel, the car taking the road in rough licks, so distressed by the transition from Jersey to New York you can almost feel it burning through the fuel. Of course I can't help but think about the night our route was reversed, when Rebecca's name emerged in LED, my thumb above *Decline*. When we were high and inoculated against embarrassment, the car crooked at the curb as he pulled me up the stairs. But when you have nights like those, anomalies where all the stars defer, and you are not faking, not even a little, the polite thing is to never mention it again. Eric reaches into the glove compartment and retrieves a flask.

"Do you understand that this is not okay? This is my family," he says, taking a long drink. I watch him, count the seconds during which his eyes are closed. For a moment, the car veers onto the shoulder. "I don't owe you anything. I was clear. I have a life, a job, a wife—"

"A child. A child who is black."

"What does it matter if she's black?"

"You could've mentioned it."

"I didn't mention it because it doesn't matter. My family is off limits."

"And your wife. Jesus."

"She wasn't always like that."

"What are you doing? Don't defend your wife to me."

"Marriage is hard," he says without any conviction, like it is something he's rehearsed.

"So hard that you can't respond to a text?"

"This is the thing with your generation. Everything is always now. There was a time when you could not reach everyone all the time."

"Maybe my life isn't as serious as yours. But I'm a person."

"You're no more a person to me than I am to you."

"What?"

"I mean I am *of use* to you. I take you out, and for another night you are spared from trying to hold a conversation with a boy your age."

"I don't need you."

"Of course you don't, that's the fucking point," he says, turning the wrong way onto a one-way street. Luckily the stretch is short, and we turn onto my block, my building looming in the city fog.

"We adopted her two years ago. She's really struggling and I don't know what to do," he says as we pull up to the curb. I think about Akila—her big, watchful eyes. The way she moved through the party, an invisible girl.

"I'm sorry," I say, and he looks over at me, his face flushed.

"I'm sorry I said I loved you. I feel awful about that."

"It's not a big deal. I didn't take it seriously."

"It had been a while for me." He pauses, slides the key out of the ignition. "You're wearing my wife's dress."

"Yeah. Is that weird for you?"

"Not weird, just—" He traces a seam in the dress thoughtfully, and it feels weird to me, the idea that he understands this dress better than I do. "I feel like I want to hurt you," he says suddenly, thumbing the collar of the dress.

"What do you mean?"

"I mean I'd like to hit you."

"Okay."

"What do you mean?"

"I mean, okay," I say, and it's odd how he rolls up his sleeve, the premeditation of it, the procedural flexing of his hand that makes it feel like he has already thought it through. And no guidelines have been established per se, but somehow I just know to present my face, to close my eyes. When the first blow comes, I feel it in my ears before I feel it anywhere else, the roots of my eyeballs curling, the general feeling like my head is sitting on a single pivot, like an owl. I bring my hand up to my cheek, almost out of expectation that the pain be concentrated here, but in a way, it is everywhere.

"Again," I say, and this time it is harder. This time I keep my eyes open and admire his focus, whatever high or extremely low regard of me is moving him to use such force. Because it is a little impolite how gamely he satisfies this request. No doubt or initial softness, just his wide, rough palm and all the liquid centers of my teeth. And this whole time we have both had our seat belts on, but he unhooks his and I unhook mine, and I look around to make sure the street is free of police and slide into his lap, where I yank the lever and recline him all the way down, this old car and its trappings made foremost to take the air out of any sexual moment, his nose in my eye as the seat flattens swiftly from 90 to 180 degrees, his cry as I hike up his wife's impossible dress, finish him, and promptly eject myself from the car. I unzip the dress before I climb the stairs so that when I reach my door I am already halfway out. I sit naked in my room and eat half a rotisserie chicken with my hands. I open my phone and find a voicemail from a number I don't recognize. While I am prepared for the voice to be hers, I am not prepared for her familiarity. I am not prepared to hear her say my name, the minor background chaos warping her voice when she says, softly, *I enjoyed meeting you, let's do that again.*

4

Here is how my mother met the man I call my father.

Grandma was a sheltered southern belle from Kentucky. The sort of high-yellow woman who believed her fair complexion was the result of an errant Native American gene, but who was, like so many of us, walking proof of American industry, the bolls and ships and casual sexual terrorism that put a little cream in the coffee and made her family loyal to the almighty paper bag.

That is to say, my grandmother was cautious about fraternizing with dark-skinned men. But then she took a typing gig in Queens and met my grandfather, a West Indian cad who was fresh off the boat. He was a gifted pianist with double-jointed fingers, a natural mimic whose classical training was just a dot over the *i*, a scrawl on a tea-stained island certificate that got him off the boat and government-approved. He saw my grandmother coming out of the Woolworth's one day and that was that. Against the wishes of her family, she darkened the line and gave him eleven children. My mother was number six, smack-dab in the middle of a transition from tall, blue-black boys to bodacious, kinky-haired girls.

There were plenty of reasons to be worried about my grand-father. The most pressing of which being the devastating charm of the Classic Trinidadian Man. The lore slants a little differ-ently depending on the island, but the conventional wisdom holds that there is no man more equipped to ruin a woman's life. By ruin, I mean it both ways, as in, ruin (/roo-in/) *noun* 1. The total disintegration of your hopes and dreams, fantastic carnage (see Pompeii) or 2. The inability of any man to com-pare (Ex. Don Omar has ruined me for other men. Ex. Niggas!). Trinidadian men do not just have eyelashes for days, they have something more subliminal that does not make itself known to you until it is nuclear and you are stuck with eleven kids in Jamaica, Queens, while he is tickling ivories for a traveling circus.

That is to say, Granddad disappeared. My mother had as good a childhood as one can have with ten brothers and sisters, sleeping three to a bunk, ushering a collection of feral alley cats into hidey-holes Grandma could not hope to find, one link in a massive West Indian brood that year by year was proving to take after my grandfather's side, meaning they were prone to disastrous dalliances with the arts and the things that make the fiscal wasteland of the arts worth the risk—the sex and drugs.

At sixteen, my uncle Pierre would die in a flophouse in Crown Heights cradling his trombone. At twenty-three, my aunt Claudia would emerge from a small Harlem cult talking about active galactic nuclei and the benefits of Himalayan crystal and tumble onto the tracks of an uptown D. Others would do okay, move to Sweden and Cape Town to sing opera and paint erotic renditions of driftwood, but my mother would take a different tack. She would take her body—this dark, powerful, curvaceous thing—and wield it all about town. After Grandma kicked her out of the house for general promiscuity and insolence, my mother would deal subpar narcotics from Bushwick to Sheepshead Bay, reinforcing the calluses on her large, archless feet with the occasional trek to a supplier in Connecticut, where she had a girlfriend who did not like to get high alone. And per this girlfriend, gradually my mother did less dealing and more using until she was strung out, living on a diet of cream soda and Greek men. Because for all her recklessness, she was not far gone enough to date an island man.

Until my father. A gruff ex-navy man with relaxed silver hair and gold fillings in his teeth. A man who spotted my mother in a bar and bankrolled a stint in rehab where she found Jesus and got clean. It wasn't until after they moved upstate and settled at a small Seventh-day Adventist church that my mother noticed his deliberation. The way he would stand before the mirror and practice his smile. The way he was exact and vain, particular about the creases in his trousers and the part in his hair. As he dressed for church, he rehearsed his testimony under his breath. He weighed each word carefully and searched for the most effective places to apply stress. Like a comedian, he came prepared to handle the fickle demands of a room; in church, these rooms were full of women. They leaned toward my father, awed by his grisly accounts of war. They competed fiercely for his favor, and he happily indulged the most vulnerable ones. By then, my mother was already a husk of herself, and I was seven years old, looking how I will always look, which is like I have a single biological parent, like my father has had no part in my creation, which, in a way, is the truth.

When I get up in the morning, I look in the mirror and I see only my mother's face. But the fact of our resemblance is such old news that to recognize it anew feels pointed, overly Freudian, a remnant of a dream I am still half inside. When she died, of course I was given to dissecting my face in the bathroom of Friendly's, or avoiding my face altogether in Macy's dressing rooms lest trying on jeans become any more demoralizing. But now I am seven years removed and there are some days I don't even think about her, though on these days a siren will keen from the end of DeKalb and it will be 3:00 a.m. and a cloud outside my window will constrict into the shape of a lung and I will hear her voice.

This morning I look in the mirror and find a bruise that makes the resemblance more pronounced, and it makes my bowels a little shy. I retreat to my room, where I kill a few roaches, take a few pictures of my face, and do some quick acrylic studies. I have never been able to finish a self-portrait, but in these studies, in the burnt sienna and purple that is meant to be my face, I see the bruises clearly, and it fills me with relief. On the train, I listen to Rebecca's voicemail over and over again. I arrive at the office with the intonations memorized. My plan for the day is to confirm the pub date for a new title about a vain giraffe and then fall down an internet rabbit hole of Rebecca Walkers who raise the dead.

My routine is always the same. I dart from the train and immediately wash my hands in the office bathroom. I load up on the free hand lotion the publisher started putting out after it was revealed that the women in the company (a whopping 87 percent of the employee base) are still making less than the men. The hand lotion has slightly increased morale, even though the quality is on par with that diabolical drugstore cocoa butter that leaves you ashier than before. I post a joke about the L train on Twitter, and I delete it when I don't get any likes. I listen to a newly pregnant publicity assistant retch (lately always between 9:03 and 9:15) in one of the stalls, and I firm up my ponytail. I kill a roach in the kitchen, grab a cup of tepid coffee, and sit at my desk, where, before I start work, I browse through some photos of friends who are doing better than me, then an article on a black teenager who was killed on 115th for holding a weapon later identified as a showerhead, then an article on a black woman who was killed on the Grand Concourse for holding a weapon later identified as a cell phone, then I drown myself in the comments section and do some online shopping, by which I mean I put four dresses in my cart as a strictly theoretical exercise and then let the page expire.

Then I start work. I look through the Tuesday publications, confirm jacket copy, triage my inbox for panicked emails from production assistants and editors trying to soothe anxious authors with quick TOC and index corrections. Details so minute as to be absurd, an em dash, the romanization of a quotation mark, a last-minute change in the acknowledgments from *I would like to thank my wife* to *I would like to thank my dog,* but, and maybe this is surprising, I am good at all of this. Arguably it would be hard to be bad at it, but if a person comes to rote work with the expectation that she will be demeaned, she can bypass the pitfalls of hope and redirect all that energy into being a merciless drone. She can be the ear for the author who calls frequently to chat about the fineries of ichthyology depicted in his series about a bullied flounder, and she can wage war with large corporate vendors whose algorithms sweep book files for errors but have huge blind spots for the speculative lexicon of science fiction, and she can say to them: This is not an error; this is human; this is style.

Today at the office, the air is still. At my desk, something is different. My manager's eyes, which, because of the open office arrangement, I can never seem to avoid, move quickly away from me. The editorial assistants are too alert, engaged in the performance of work. Then Aria comes in with a box of doughnuts. This would be cause to celebrate, except the person who helps her through the door is Mark. I see his hand, his desecrated fingernails and large knuckles, and I turn away and look into the dark face of my phone, which reflects a bruised iteration of my face. It occurs to me that I should've covered it up, but more pressing is the reality in which Aria and Mark just happen to be having the sort of conversations that spill into other rooms, because I'm certain they have nothing in common and no overlapping professional tasks.

I eavesdrop on them, which in an open plan is not eavesdropping so much as accepting your silent role in everyone's conversation, and they are talking about a comic book I can't place, Mark doing this thing where he prefaces every one of his observations with *what you need to understand is*, Aria's breathless reception of these condescensions so pure and sweet. When he is gone, I try to make meaningful eye contact with Aria, but she will not indulge. I try to find Rebecca on the internet, but there is a

new message from HR. Early August is generally when employee evaluations start, and I have prepared a diplomatic way
to say that I loathe everyone here, but the message does not
seem to be about this. It is a vaguely worded invitation for a
meeting at 4:00 p.m.

I step outside and smoke a joint, and there are interns everywhere, beaming and overdressed and happy to be paid in
experience. I wonder if I have looked too miserable at my
desk, if I forgot to use a private browser when I was active on
SugarBabees.com. Anyone could do my job with the proper
training, and if I fell down the escalator of the Times Square
Forever 21 and severed my spine it would not make office
news.

I grab a doughnut and arrive at the meeting with two minutes
to spare. The HR rep smiles at me and asks me to close the
door. My boss, a squirrelly little editor who came up in sales
and frequently lurks behind me after her bathroom breaks in
an attempt to peer at my screen, is seated next to him. I smile
at her and try to pretend that she is not pro-life. I lean forward
to show my engagement and try to summon the spirit of the
Grateful Diversity Hire. They start out with a few compliments, which I receive readily. Yes, I've whipped the digital
archive into shape. Yes, I delivered on the K–5 Maya Angelou
and Frida Kahlo biographies, wherein the sexual assault and
bus accident were omitted per a Provo parents group who

weren't ready for their kids to see the blood women wade through to create art.

"Still, you have been on probation twice," the HR rep says, trying not to look at the bruise on my face.

"I fell off my bike in Central Park," I say, which only seems to make the bruise into a bigger deal. My boss and the HR rep glance at each other. "And yes, I completed two probationary periods, but the second time there was sort of a misunderstanding. HorseGirls .com was a link featured in one of our middle-grade ebooks, but domains tend to change over time. A parent called about the adult content, and I just wanted to do my due diligence," I say, and my boss coughs, though it is one of those snide, performative coughs that most people stop doing after the age of twelve. I can't think of a single moment she has ever been straightforward with me, and, even now, she redirects the conversation with words like *tolerance* and *inclusivity* before the HR rep cuts to the chase and says that some men and women in the company feel I've been sexually inappropriate. They are both being very sensitive about it, clearly upset by the optics of the whole thing, bracketing what is happening in such carefully neutral language that in a way, I feel sorry for them. And what is happening is that I'm getting fired. There are emails. Pictures sent over company servers. Complaints about which they are not permitted to offer any details.

There are a few encounters that come to mind, ingenious anatomical feats that, sure, happened on company time. Coworkers with elaborate, transgressive fantasies that I was dead enough inside to fulfill. And, of course, there is Mark. When I try to explain, there is a tremor in my voice. I try to regain my composure, but I am sensitive to the power even of authority figures I despise. I close my eyes and will myself not to cry, but I was so close to being able to spend eleven dollars on lunch. All I can do is take the doughnut out of my purse and press it all into my mouth at once. I stand up, knowing I only have so much time before the tears, and I go to the bathroom, lock myself in a stall, and puke.

But the impulse to cry has vanished. I imagine the high traffic I will meet on my way back and try to get the tears out while I have the privacy, but nothing happens. When I go to my desk, a conversation in full swing dies abruptly as I gather my pens, unscrew the lightbulb from my desk lamp and toss it in my purse. I take some pink Post-its, my work slippers, and a legal pad where I have the beginning of a story about a wolf who can't find the right pair of glasses. Someone has left a plastic bag for me, which is such a nice gesture that for a moment, I am out of breath. But as I put my thermos of Tanqueray into the bag, I think of when I first arrived, Tom showing me how to clock in and declare PTO, and how at the end of the day I took the scenic route home, the sun in one borough, the moon in another, this desire in me to clap my hand over the lens of a tourist's camera and say, *Stop, there isn't enough time.*

I feel everyone in the room can see these two versions of me, like a before and after. In the after, I am even fatter. I want to say something before I leave, but I've never been good at parting words and the pressure makes me nervous, so I say *Please invite me to lunch sometime* to the one assistant I like best. As I leave, I really wish I could take it back.

I go back to the bathroom and try to cry again. When nothing happens I listen to Rebecca's voicemail and press the bruise on my face. I think of Eric's slack, hungry face, the thrill of pulling my body from his and shutting the car door, which is maybe what it feels like to have the last word. I want to believe this is intolerable to him, but he hasn't been in contact. I text him and say *miss you*, and when I see the ellipses on my phone, I can tell that he has opened the message and is beginning to reply. But then he doesn't, and so I take a slug of gin and head to Mark's office.

Even with the necessary lubrication, I find myself paralyzed in the stairwell, thinking of reasons not to go up to his floor. I find myself becoming sentimental about what I will leave behind, the whiff of Lysol and ink, the stack of someone's homemade zines on the sink, and this very stairwell, in which I have regularly pleaded for student loan deferrals and set up pelvic exams. I have said goodbye enough times to know that departure has a way of gilding what are, at best, slow quotidian deaths, but still each time I think of everything I will lose.

—————

When I walk into his office, for a while he proceeds as if I'm not there. He leafs through a fat folder of proofs, jots down something on his Wacom, and leans back in his chair with a lukewarm smile. He is cool, which is very out of the ordinary. A departure from his usual frequency—a distinctly uncool vibration that once engaged is effusive to the point of violence, a nerd's nerd so smitten with the niche corners of eighties ephemera and pan-Asian iconography that his office, like his apartment, is a precarious collection of teacups, toys, and squat fertility figurines. The effort behind his demeanor should put me at ease, but actually it hurts. And this is not how I expected to feel. I close the door and take his katana off the wall.

"Do you remember when we went to Brighton Beach? It was maybe the only time you and I went outside together."

"Please put that back. It's ceremonial."

"There was a used condom in the sand. And it rained. I slipped on the boardwalk and I was embarrassed. You don't know this, but I had done a great deal of preparation the night before. Because you had only ever seen me in the dark."

"Muromachi era," he says, and behind him is a large print of *The Great Wave off Kanagawa*, the tallest wave cradling the shiny crown of his head. When I unsheathe the blade, it makes such a satisfying sound that I do it again.

"I got fired today."

"What?"

"Don't do that. Act like it wasn't you."

"You think I got you fired? Edie, baby."

"I never said no to you. Not to anything. That documentary about Norwegian puppetry was three hours long."

"Listen, I have been on probation since the late aughts, okay? I have nothing to gain in telling anyone about what happened with us," he says, and I turn the katana over in my hands. The weight is concentrated toward the hilt, which briefly destabilizes me. All at once the color and grain of the room distill into high focus, and I note the old shaving scar beneath his lip at the same time I note the seriousness of the blade, which I assumed would be dulled.

"I did everything you asked. Even that thing with the *tengu* mask."

"My love, this is the problem with your generation. Instant gratification," he says, and because it took him, on average, forty-three minutes to come, because I put on the ears and the tail and learned the lyrics to "Painting the Roses Red" backward and forward, because I drank approximately five gallons of cranberry juice over the course of our relationship, and for a day or two required the use of a cane, I take issue with his definition of *instant*. Though there is still a part of me that is vulnerable to his casual use of *my love*, which, when we were together, appeared without warning at the end of his requests for me to get the door and pass the remote. "You think you should get what you want, when you want it, and life doesn't work that way. Art doesn't work that way, and that's why you're not as good as you could be," he says, and the fact that he doesn't appear to have said this in anger, the fact of him offering this insult as practical advice, is something I feel in the most inaccessible parts of my bowels. So he may not be the reason for my sudden unemployment. In the wake of this possibility are dozens of new culprits, minor office affairs all about the building, but there are too many to parse, and so I take the katana, maneuver the blade between my fingers, and press it down into the flesh. Directly after the act comes a clarity so sharp it feels enhanced, the room ballooning such that his shout reaches me belatedly as I squeeze my hand into a fist and watch the blood well between my fingers. And even then, I feel nothing. But when I look at the carpet, the spot there is excellent, is proof, spreading into the shape of a smile.

I take the elevator down with two publicists, my hand pressed into a work slipper. They are craned over a list of pub dates, talking about a galley at the center of the third scandal of the year. It is a highly designed editorial nightmare from a boutique imprint experimenting with pomo cookbooks, formerly an imprint that specialized in Crock-Pot tips and a series on pies that employed the authority of a titular Presbyterian Grandma. To sex up the brand, they invited a popular chef, known for his radical liquid nitrogen ice cream, to write a cookbook. Except then his wife went missing and someone found her frozen foot.

In the lobby, there is a Diversity Giveaway. I go up to the table and scan the books, and there are a few new ones: a slave narrative about a mixed-race house girl fighting for a piece of her father's estate; a slave narrative about a runaway's friendship with the white schoolteacher who selflessly teaches her how to read; a slave narrative about a tragic mulatto who raises the dead with her magic chitlin pies; a domestic drama about a black maid who, like Schrödinger's cat, is both alive and dead, an unseen, nurturing presence who exists only within the bounds of her employer's four walls; an "urban" romance where everybody dies by gang violence; and a book about a Cantonese restaurant, which may or may not have been written by a white woman from Utah, whose descriptions of her characters rely primarily on rice-based foods. I take the book by the white woman and head outside, where Aria is leaning against the building, smoking a cigarette. She casts a bored glance in my direction, reaches into her bag and pulls out another cigarette. I take it, accept her light.

"They're giving me your job," she says, smoke streaming from her nose.

"I know," I say, even though it is only now that I look at her soft, dark profile and feel that I have been swapped out for a prettier, more docile model.

"I know what you're thinking," she says, and around her eyes is the residue of old mascara, which against her usual prim white cardigan is more disturbing to me than the homeless man who is urinating next to us. "You think I'm a coon."

"I don't think that." Of course I do think that, but now that she's said it out loud and I see the look on her face, I feel bad.

"We could've been friends. I really needed a friend here," she says, turning to toss the cigarette. I can see the clips mounting her synthetic yaki ponytail. Though I have in the past taken such poor care of my hair I've had to shave my head to preempt inevitable baldness, I want to take her face into my hands and point her in the direction of a good wig store. I would prefer to be upset with her, but my hand is bleeding profusely, and this is precisely her charm, the reason the professional whites talk openly to her about their fiscal conservatism—her lovely brown doll face, her full mouth and kind, carefully empty eyes.

I don't know if there is any good way to admit my own desire without seeming deranged, because this hypothetical in which we were friends was never purely hypothetical to me. The blossoming and immediate kibosh of our friendship had in fact taken me months of half-written emails to get over. Because it is impossible to see another black woman on her way up, impossible to see that meticulous, polyglottal origami and not, as a black woman yourself, fall a little bit in love. But we had nothing at all in common.

"Please. I was a liability to you," I say, holding the smoke in the back of my throat.

"Well. Yes." She lights another cigarette, smiles. "But not like you think."

"You're going to tell me again what I think?"

"You think because you slack and express no impulse control that you're like, black power. Sticking it to the white man or whatever. But you're just exactly what they expect. Like, I understand wanting to resist their demands. But they can be mediocre. We can't."

"Mediocre?"

"I can't be associated with it. Like, there is actually a brief window where they don't know to what extent you're black, and you have to get in there. You have to get in the room. And if I have to, I will shuck and jive until the room I'm in is at the top."

———

It is only once I am underground that the arteries in my hand truly begin to weep. It is one of those early August days where the oxygen in the air is uncoupled, dense with Drakkar Noir, old pollen, and reheated Spam. It is one of those days where the M is full of Italian tourists energized from a full day at Banana Republic, and three stops in, my sweat is their sweat, the pores on Federico's neck emptying into my mouth. There is blood everywhere, and I can at least count on my city not to notice, though a baby by the door is pointing at me, so I turn away and try to look involved with my phone. Then, in the brief window of service between Manhattan and Brooklyn, Eric sends me a photo of a friar fleeing a baboon. He writes, *at this archival conference in toronto and saw this illuminated text. pages are swollen, binding is beyond reinforcement. this thing is nearing the end of its life. you can practically smell the rot.*

Having already been in the process of filing him away, burying him with the other men who evaporate after pulverizing my cervix, I am relieved, and yes, I am ashamed. I want to say that I am not that kind of girl. Portable, contorting herself over an inaccessible, possibly disinterested man, but what if I am? There are worse things—factory farming and Christian rock and the three-dimensional animation of Mr. Clean. Because maybe I don't want to be cool. Maybe I want to be all-purpose. Maybe I can't pretend to be aloof to men who are aloof to me. So I text him two hundred words' worth of things I know about baboons and I play Rebecca's voicemail again with this exchange still fresh.

———

When I arrive home I can't extend my fingers, and the floor moves when I open the door. By that I mean we have roaches and they scatter as I search for some peroxide and gauze. But of course we don't have these things. We don't even have a smoke detector. For instance, we have a big general pill bottle where we keep some old ibuprofen, Xanax, and Alka-Seltzer, we have some coconut oil we use for bacon and our hair, and for cutlery, three butter knives, one of which keeps showing up in the shower. Neither I nor my roommate is very prepared, which is why we get along and then have huge fights in the case of there being an actual emergency, usually re: the mice.

So I rinse my hand after washing it with a little Irish Spring, and I look for some toilet paper, but we are out. I look for a T-shirt to wrap my hand in, but I have no clean clothes and have been putting off doing laundry by wearing my bathing suit as underwear. So I find some raw canvas in the back of my closet, wrap it around my hand, and take my paintings out with the trash.

I stop at the corner grocery, spend $5.65 on a package of good, soft toilet paper and $3.89 on a large, store-brand carrot cake. I consider buying a box of Band-Aids, but even the generic brand costs more than I want to spend. I strip down to my bikini and stop by the laundromat, where I spend $3.25 on a standard wash and dry and make a few calls about my student loans. I portion out my last paychecks on the back of my hand with a Sharpie while the rinse cycle goes, and something about how this arithmetic sprawls down my arm makes me feel like I can make it work. When I return home, a mouse has started on my carrot cake, so I make some instant oatmeal and retreat to my room, where I listen to my roommate and her feminist boyfriend having very sweet communicative sex.

I work on my résumé, slip in a vague communications role peddling paraben-free dog shampoo, and, to show I have character, I stick to the facts regarding my month at Murray's, where I mongered an array of soft cheese. I throw in some blatant lies and make sure any inconsistencies are small enough to explain away once I have a foot in the door and am armed with enough recon on my interviewer to either have talking points on the company culture or a five-point plan to suck dry any available reservoirs of white guilt. I interview well despite my nerves, and while I wish I could take credit for that, my ability to maintain human form and make a good impression is all about my skin. The expectations of me in these settings are frequently so low, it would be impossible not to surpass them. I send a few applications out, wrap my hand in some fresh toilet paper, and for a few hours I manage to sleep.

I have a dream about the bones in my skull liquefying, and when I wake up and see my laundry basket, something about the inevitability of dirty clothes, of the sebum and discharge, of a finite number of quarters, fills me with panic. And this is not so bad. Some nights I lie awake and the sky presents an entire anatomy that makes me feel hopeless and sometimes like a spider is crawling across my face, but tonight feels different. Tonight I am suspended in a lurid hypnagogic loop in which the ground is always rushing upward, the Japanese demon squatting on my chest lengthening to its full height, peeling back its long buttocks to reveal a fully functioning eye.

I think of my parents, not because I miss them, but because sometimes you see a black person above the age of fifty walking down the street, and you just know that they have seen some shit. You know that they are masters of the double consciousness, of the discreet management of fury under the tight surveillance and casual violence of the outside world. You know that they said thank you as they bled, and that despite the roaches and the instant oatmeal and the bruise on your face, you are still luckier than they have ever been, such that losing a bottom-tier job in publishing is not only ridiculous but offensive.

In the morning, no jobs have contacted me, but there is a text from Eric accompanied by a photo of a fully erect seraphim. He writes, *take a look at that grass. the color is called verdigris and they used to make it by boiling copper in vinegar,* and I don't respond because I can't bring myself to do anything but get up to go to the bathroom, and even that is something I have to convince myself to do, because I have not once wet myself in adulthood and I think perhaps I'm due. A couple of days after that, I put some water in a glass and drink it, and Eric sends me a picture of a chimera with a star-shaped tongue. He writes, *in the tradition of grotteschi. the art of the grotesque. But how cool is this. in the beginning grotteschi just meant ornate,* and I send out a few more job applications and take a shower. I start to shave my legs, but on the second leg the lights turn off and I stand there in the dark with the razor, feeling like the universe is suggesting something. Eric texts me more photos of gargoyles and vagina dentata and no jobs call back even when I revise my résumé daily and spend $28.09 at Marshalls on a pantsuit.

By the time I feel able to contribute to our conversation, it becomes obvious that it is not a conversation. It becomes obvious that he does not intend to acknowledge punching me in the face or the terrible, revelatory night I spent at his home. The texts come intermittently and without any prompting, though Eric usually sends them at around noon and midnight, which tells me that I occur to him during lunch and perhaps while he is still in bed. In between these texts, I want to ask him what he's eating. I want to ask him why he is awake. But then I worry he'll remember I'm on the other end and the texts will stop. This is the way it was when our relationship only existed online. We told each other things so awful that by necessity we adopted the posture of speaking in jest, though we had gone through the trouble to create a language, and the effort of this alone betrayed our seriousness. And then we met. Then I got into his car and had to recalibrate, give him eyelashes and veins under his hands and a freckle on his chin, and suddenly it seemed indecent to acknowledge any of the things we'd said. And so when he texts a photo of a satyr being skinned and says, *dig the saffron and gold leaf. we use a synthetic compound to counteract the pores*, I say nothing.

Some days later I snag an interview for a corporate gig in Long Island City, but when I get there, it is just a staffing firm and the woman I meet with tells me she has a client looking for a waste management associate. When I show up to the dump, the mid-August heat is so relentless that the creases I ironed into my pants melt away. By the time I arrive in the main office I've reverted to a liquid state, my interviewer asking me how much I can haul, to which I respond with an overestimation of about fifty pounds, the vibe in the room a little bit Ku Klux until I go to the bathroom and see that for the length of the interview my mascara has been running and there are big black tears still making their way down my cheeks. This is something I want to tell Eric, but because of our gaping economic disparity, I don't know how to express myself without it seeming like I'm asking for help.

So I send my social security number to an email linked to an office in Silicon Valley where a popular in-app delivery system is based. In three days they send me a hat and a carrier bag with thermal insulation to keep the deliveries warm. They grant me access to a map that shows the areas of the city with the highest demand. Heavily populated areas show up dark red, and less populated areas tend to remain pink, until lunchtime, when demand is high even in the sleepy hamlets of Queens. I ride my bike to an address in Sunset Park and when the customer comes to the door, she snatches the bag of waffle fries and doesn't tip. Most of the time, I stay in Brooklyn. I get the first orders of no-pulp orange juice and champagne out of the way. Make pit stops for vanilla Juul pods, small orders of LaCroix and Pampers. I make my home base Holy Cross Cemetery so I can hydrate in relative peace, and also because it's smack-dab in the middle of Flatbush, the orders come in from all sides. Technically, I'm not allowed to transport anything that qualifies as a drug, but there are prep school kids who need bubble tea and Marlboros, dog walkers who need boxed wine and leave detailed instructions about where in Prospect to make the drop, pump-and-dumping mommies who emerge from the Grand Army market, desperate for gin. Everyone is excited to see me, and I am sort of excited to see them, the habitual Bensonhurst McFlurries, the Gen X brownstoners who, for some reason, use the app to order pizza, Coney Islanders looking to indulge in brunch from afar and are just happy you came out, the West Indian pockets of Eastern Parkway and their cash-only ackee and coco bread, beaucoup tips on the days I wear the company hat and beat the average time, though occasionally I take the bridge over and field requests by Canal, where I try to protect orders of squid from all that direct sun.

But for all the visits I make, they never go beyond hello. I try to segue from light observations about the weather, and in the few who are receptive, between my strict schedule of work and sleep, I find I don't have the bandwidth to offer anything more. So I listen to NPR on my route to try to get some talking points. I find a segment about a journalist who received a string of violent emails in 2009. The journalist reads part of one email and laughs. *He wrote to me on the first of every month, and he would say these things, like you ‹redacted› whore how do men find your ‹redacted›, and I felt like, it's not even constructive. If you have an issue with my reporting, okay.* Then they bring the man who sent the emails on air, and he says, *I'm sorry, I was having a rough year.*

If I go home, it is usually for the bathroom I know and love, though there is a mom-and-pop Thai joint in Gravesend with a sterling private restroom, and they are so grateful for how much geng kheaw wan gai I move that they let me use it for free. I try not to take any deliveries with a high probability of soup, and I try to obey traffic laws, though sometimes there is a wedding, a parade, or a murder that forces me to rush and leave my bike in an illegal place. With a new diet of pear baby food and Top Ramen, I make almost enough money to live, though some of that is due to my payout from the publisher. Then I receive news that my rent is going up. The news comes in a brown, grease-stained envelope, and because usually I only receive mail from student loan consolidation scams and instant-approval credit card companies that use old rap icons to target low-income blacks, I almost miss it. My roommate calls a meeting while I'm out falling from my bike into a customer's cheesecake, and as soon as I climb the stairs she is there with a suitcase, saying she's moving to a gut-renovated building in Harlem with her boyfriend as *send me a picture of your pussy* pings onto my screen.

As I watch my roommate leave, the idea that I have a pussy seems preposterous. I move through the apartment and try to reconcile the existence of the clitoris with the broccoli smell my roommate left behind. I rinse the cheesecake from my hair and get back out on my route, where the men who line the street remind me that technically yes, I do have a pussy, and that I will live with the terror of protecting it for the rest of my life. But after a big haul of spices from Halal Food I go ahead and take a picture of it in the bathroom of an Au Bon Pain. Then I go back to my newly empty apartment, google utility-free SROs in the Bronx, and introduce some saline to my anal cavity. I watch *Seinfeld*, comb Jason Alexander's IMDb, and head to Manhattan to make a little more cash. I bike the Queensboro Bridge, and mop my face and armpits in the bathroom of a Pret. I check the delivery map and uptown is already deep red, a swath of demand from Harlem to Fifty-Ninth and Lex for the matcha, mylk, and hemp offerings of corporate, quirky, or decidedly snide coffee giants, the bike lanes in Manhattan already terrifying at 11:00 a.m., filled with delivery boys and girls who jet into traffic with fried rice and no reason to live, along with the sentient abdominals who do this for fun, foreign pedestrians standing right in the way, taking selfies and checking their luggage for pigeon shit.

As far as Eric is concerned, there is no genital reciprocity. He sends a photo of himself holding a vial of powdered silver, and despite his general old man-ness regarding the art of the selfie and his dorky archival gloves, I want him. I have been waiting for a reason to rescind my attraction. I hoped in the two weeks we have been apart, I could be objective and find something wrong with him. But after this month, all I want is to be kissed. I ask my customers to confirm my name, at times to be sure I have the right address, but mostly just to hear the sound.

Five bundles of kale for a customer in an eighth-floor walkup in Flatiron. A vial of rosewater for a customer in Greenwich Village whose labradoodle humps me down the stairs. Band-Aids and cigarillos for a customer who runs out of the Strand with a stiletto clutched in each hand. Chipotle every which way and always with no beans. Three black wigs made of virgin Malaysian hair for a half-human, half-turquoise customer on Bowery, soggy Chelsea mailwomen with their tired, roving eyes, white drug dealers in Sperrys waving to the NYPD, delivery people properly affiliated with pizza parlors and flower shops all hooked into the peripheral intuition that keeps us all from falling into the city's bounty of open holes. Though now I walk over a subway grate and am excited by the possibility of its giving way, because despite the city's breakneck, multilingual carousel,

despite the businessmen marching into my path and the ellipti-
cal assault of glass and steel and scary wooden trains in Upper
East Side toy stores, I don't feel like I'm moving even while I'm
on my feet, up and down and in and out and pressing a dollar
slice directly into my large intestine, my parking jobs incremen-
tally more careless as the orders come one, two, six, as I exit a
sad Central Park studio at 12:53 a.m. and find my bike not gone
per se but divorced from both its wheels. So I take my basket
and my bell and hold them in my lap on the F, the L, and the
posthumous fart that is the B60 bus, asleep before I fall into bed
and then rise to my landlord-cum-yogi sucking an appetite-
suppressant lollipop in my doorway, asking me to pay up or get
out, and also namaste, before I take a cold shower and pay for
one of those gargantuan Citi Bikes, which tend not to be made
for girls under five foot two and so tend not to be conducive to
punctual deliveries or preventing you from careening into someone's gazpacho or sprawling into a four-way intersection, ready
to surrender the part of yourself that M train mariachi hasn't
already killed.

I wake up to a group of surly Elmhurst Slavs putting my stuff
out on the curb and find myself, at 7:00 a.m., embroiled in an
argument over my toaster oven, which necessitates that I take a
Lyft to a storage facility in Bedford Park. The city is coming up
pink on my map, all tapped out despite a torrential downpour
that has cleared the streets. A lone woman darts from the subway with a plastic bag over her head, an umbrella salesman
looks over his table and sucks his teeth, and a river cuts down

Great Jones, but otherwise it is one of those rare nights where everyone is inside with all the right condiments and drugs, and I am obsolete. I go a little lower to try to get some work. I stand in front of a few popular pickup spots and wait. I go inside for some water, and because the waitstaff know me, they give me some gnocchi alla vodka on the house. They treat me like a customer. I get a folded cloth napkin, and they come around with the parmesan. It is sort of a joke, because I still have my helmet on and my map open. But then I look at the food, and I look around the empty restaurant, and I lose my appetite. I apologize and take the Citi Bike a little ways uptown to get some air, but it doesn't help. I feel like I'm wearing a lead apron, like each of my limbs, one by one, is falling asleep. On my map, I note two bridges within biking distance. Then the first order of the day comes in. It is a standard supermarket run, though when I get to the store and scroll down the list (cotton balls, crunchy peanut butter, lobster bisque from the hot bar) I see there is a request that I go to a second location, an army navy on Forty-Fifth, and purchase a small Stryker bone saw.

In the grocery store, there are only three other people, and one of them is a cashier. I pass a woman in the seafood section, and she smiles at me, but beneath her smile I see her wondering where everyone is. I feel our silliness, my reliance on the city's density, which I have spent so much time hating but proves to be the last barrier between me and some inconceivable boss-level of concentrated loneliness. As I ladle the bisque into a cup,

I try to focus solely on the soup and not on my teeth, my skin, and the gradual breakdown of my body into dust. At the army navy store, the salesman doesn't ask any questions, and I don't regret the purchase until I'm halfway to my destination, which turns out to be a hospital. But a quarter mile out, a car speeds through a stop sign and I stop short and spill all the bisque. At this point in my career, I can deliver almost any bad news about soup, but when I get to the entrance, I notice that some of the lobster has gotten into my shoes, just as Rebecca comes jogging out of the hospital in scrubs and rubber boots. For a moment I think maybe I can wring out my socks before she reaches me, but it is too late. If she is shocked, I see no sign of it on her face. She takes off her gloves and looks through the bags. She inspects the saw and sighs. She asks me to come inside. So I go with her through the waiting room, every bodily fluid already detectable in the air despite the pineapple air freshener at the reception desk, where a man with a prosthetic arm begs for Percocet and a colossal goldfish hangs suspended in its own waste. We step into the elevator and Rebecca puts her hand up when I try to broach the subject of the soup.

"It doesn't matter," she says as we head into the cafeteria, where she pulls out a chair and asks me to sit down. She settles down across from me, brings out the peanut butter. She takes a spoon out of her coat and cleans it on her lapel. "Why didn't you call? I left you a voicemail," she says, opening the peanut butter, hooking her finger into the oil collecting at the top.

"I've been busy," I answer, but as I say this I think about her message, about the huskiness underneath the words, the suspicion I have that she may have been smiling. The voice she has now is different. It sounds like a voice anyone might have. "In the app it said Becky Abramov."

"Maiden name." She sucks her finger, frowns into the jar. "This is dangerous work for a woman. How can you know who'll be on the other side of the door?"

"This city isn't really dangerous anymore." As I say this, I relish the feeling of a vintage lie. A thing I would say to my father when he was alive and trying to make an effort to call. "I lost my job," I say, thinking it will feel cathartic and realizing immediately that I am wrong.

"I'm sorry about that." She pushes the peanut butter over to me, extends her spoon.

"What's the saw for?" I turn the spoon around to look at my reflection, and even though I know how the image will refract, it still takes me aback.

"I work here at the VA, as a medical examiner. The guy I have today has the hardest skull I've ever seen. My husband didn't tell you what I do?"

"We don't talk about you," I say, wondering if it will hurt her. I resent her presumption that we would talk about her at all until I see her disappointment.

"We talk about you," she says, and I get the feeling that I'm meant to ask what about, so I don't. But I want to know. I want to know what he's said, and when she smiles I know she can see it on my face.

"And you like that? Hearing about what we do?"

"It's not that I like it. But I like to be informed. Control for variables. I know that's not your thing."

"How would you know?"

"Because you don't care who's on the other side of the door." She pauses and looks at me, her eyes distant, studious. "Let me show you something," she says, screwing the top back on the jar and striding to the elevator, which is papered in flyers that say things like: *Need Help? Did the war come back home with you?*

We go to the floor below basement parking. We step into a room awash with fluorescent light, and it looks like the pre-owned section of Ikea, everything straightforward but a little lopsided, a small desk strewn with sheaves of that pink, perforated paper, a lone computer chair with no arms, a small calcified shower in the corner. She rifles through a plastic bin and brings out a gray Tyvek suit. "Here, put this on," she says, shrugging off her white coat. She ties up her hair with a plain rubber band, takes off her clothes, and steps into a suit of her own. As she does this, I notice a tattoo on the base of her neck that says *the grateful*. "You don't have to take your clothes off. I just can't tolerate the heat." It's not that I'm threatened by her body, but I am uncomfortable undressing in front of her now that I've seen it, the marbled flesh of her thighs, which, even without the assistance of clothes, appear to go all the way up to her neck, her depressing beige bra and high-waisted underwear with *Wednesday* on the back. Her complete nonchalance at being seen like this. I've exposed my body for nothing. For a tip, for lunch, for a hand attached to a man I couldn't see. But now I take the suit and feel it is insufficient to have hand-washed my underwear. I feel her taking inventory of where her husband has been. I keep my clothes on and step into the suit. She hands me a mask, says, "Activated charcoal," and pops two batteries into a transistor radio. She washes her hands and pulls on a pair of purple gloves. She tells me to take the radio, and when I turn up the dial a silky voice says *nothing but Hall and Oates, and in a few, we'll take some calls.* When she rolls her neck and marches toward the metal door, I want to tell her to stop.

"Have you ever seen a cadaver?" she asks, opening the door and sweeping into the room, where the body of a black man is splayed, his scalp peeled neatly away from his skull.

"Yes, my mother," I say before I can stop it, and she pauses, somehow already deeply involved in a task that involves looping some blue rubber tubing around her arm.

"I didn't know that," she says, turning back to her task. "Does Eric know that?"

"No, he doesn't."

"That's good," she says, heaving the body to the side, clearing the waste collecting around his legs. "Keep something for yourself." She takes the cotton balls and presses them into the cadaver's anus. I try to look at the body directly. I tell myself that this is ordinary, that within me there is already a catalog of men just like this, supine, darkening the pavement, disappearing into shareable content. But it is too much to see his open mouth and genitals, the pallid bottoms of his feet.

"How did he die?"

"He got hit by a car. Family lost track of him. Dementia." She unravels the cord for the saw. "Turn the radio up, will you?" When I turn up the volume, the same voice says *a successful white ethnostate. This one is for Gerta in Williamsburg. Buckle in for "Private Eyes."* As the song starts up, she palms what is exposed of the skull. She starts the saw, lowers it to the bone.

"Why did you call me?" I ask, mostly for something to do with my mouth.

"I don't know. I think I was trying to understand it."

"What?"

"Why he would choose you," she answers quietly, most of her attention directed toward the task of positioning her hands underneath the brain. And when the brain comes out it is both smaller and less pink than I expected. She lingers, presses her finger against the seam. But from here she is all muscle memory, a moving artillery in a hazmat suit, the bone cutters and chisels and enterotomes moving in and out of her hands. Inside my suit, my body is vapor, but I don't know how to leave. I might miss something. Because of an invisible suture along an eyelid, and the damp hair against Rebecca's neck. Because in an hour, a man without a brain will be a man who looks like he can dream. We don't speak but I know I am wanted exactly where I am, holding the radio, turning it up and down against her sounds of consent, Rebecca's love for "Rich Girl" apparent in the soft tapping of her foot. We listen to the same commercials over and over again, and after she finishes, we go back into the other room. I take off my suit and change the channel to an AM station while she is showering. A voice says *accept the lord Jesus as your true* and she throws on her jacket and turns the radio off. Outside, most of the cars are gone. We share a single cigarette because she says it makes her feel like it doesn't count. She says she is aware of the irony of being a medical examiner who smokes, but that for all the blackened lungs she's seen, it is more disturbing to open the chest cavity of a veteran and find that it is pristine.

"Imagine living life so carefully that there are no signs you lived at all," she says. "I thought I was going to be a surgeon. Then my first year of med school, we got our first cadavers, and there was so much data inside. You can be sure a patient will lie about how much they drink or how much they smoke, but with a cadaver, all the information is there." She lights another cigarette and sighs. "It's like walking through a stranger's house and touching all their things."

"I'm sorry," I say, and she laughs.

"No, you're not." She looks at me for a while and starts her car from a remote on her key. I follow the headlights to a silver SUV. "You noticed our daughter. When you came to the house," she finally says, and in this moment it becomes clear to me that despite this evening-long conspiracy, she is moving toward her most natural conclusion, which is to engage me not as a person who has just watched her dissect a man but as a person who is black, and who is, because of that, available for her support.

"Yes."

"What did you think of her?"

"I don't know. She seemed fine," I say, though of course she did not seem fine. She seemed alone, like it had been years since anyone had done her hair.

"She doesn't have any friends," she says, the cigarette forgotten between her fingers.

"Oh," I say, trying to show my disinterest, but the principle of the thing doesn't prevent it from bothering me, this thing Eric failed to mention, the look in Akila's eyes as she climbed the stairs. My desire to deny Rebecca this attempt to create a link where there is none is less pressing than my embarrassment for their daughter, who may or may not be the kind of kid who wants friends, but who almost certainly would hate her mother talking about it. But then I look at Rebecca's face, and I look at her crooked cigarette, and it seems possible that the woman who chased me down the stairs and the woman who sawed through eight millimeters of skull are one and the same, a woman inclined to problem-solve by any means, so competent that any adjacent failure becomes her own. Obviously, I don't relate. I take a moment to revel in the schadenfreude, but mostly I feel suckered into admitting it, that it matters, that I have thought about it, the apparent isolation of their child, a thing immediately recognizable to me for being myself that thing which is both hypervisible and invisible: black and alone. But at the same time I resent it, I feel competitive about our respective levels of despair, and so I tell her I have nowhere to go, which I mean to say matter-of-factly, but which comes out of my mouth as a hideous and sopping thing, the bisque underneath my toenails suddenly emblematic of my serial embarrassment, which Rebecca meets unflinchingly and without a single word of condolence, smoking her cigarette and inspecting her nails. She hangs in the silence, much like the way she did post-karaoke, and then she tosses the cigarette and tells me to get in the car.

———

So I put the bike in the trunk and we drive in silence toward the nearest docking station. We head out of the city and I am smitten with the AC, the soft orange lights along the dash, the Freon and wild cherry at the center of the new car smell. The spasm of the radio frequency around Rebecca's FM preset and the long, sulfuric miles of sky beyond Weehawken, opening my eyes just as we pass through the tunnel, halfway into REM as Rebecca parks the car and walks up to the mailbox with *Walker* on the side, the act of her getting the mail such a sweet, quotidian thing that I pretend to be asleep.

She leads me up the stairs and into a guest room, where she does some business with a sheet, muttering about amenities and organic toothpaste and a neighbor's dog. I offer a dutiful laugh that comes out dry and loud, exacerbating the spectacle of our mutual effort to be casual. Because I'm aware of the breadth of the house, even as I try to take up as little space as possible. I'm aware that the room is owned, each square foot considered and likely free of mice. In this room that no one sleeps in, there is still evidence of life. Department store stills of wet cobblestone and pitted fruit, moody Helmut Newtons of smoking women, drapes the same shade of mauve my mom used to paint the kitchen the day she killed herself, furniture with the too-balanced stretch marks of the deliberately distressed, this willingness to pay for degradation something I want to hate but actually relate to, the ficus, wicker, and ornamental glass all cherries on top, a cohesive domesticity that I find weird and a little threatening, but that fills me with the yearning to retrieve my toaster oven from storage and find a place to plug it in.

That Rebecca also appears uncomfortable is comforting to me, because even as she bends over and I finally conclude that I'm better looking, I am aware of her competence, of her satisfied charity, even as she stands gravely in the doorway and says, *this is just for now,* as if she has begrudgingly accepted my presence in her house and did not in fact initiate this whole thing. She just lingers as I slip off my shoes and peel off my socks. I let my hair down and try not to feel her eyes. And then she comes back into the room. She begins to speak but looks elsewhere, wringing her hands. She says she is an evolved woman, that it is debatable whether monogamy is biologically sound, and an open marriage can be good in theory, but Eric is not great at time management and could this thing with her husband please stop. Then she leaves the room, apparently as excited as I am for the moment to be over. For a while I lie awake in the dark, wondering about how ending things with Eric might feel, and the answer is that it would feel great, not just because he's borrowed anyway, but because I would have the last word. He may be the only man in recent memory to make me come, but he is not even on Twitter. I could find someone my age. Someone my age who is clean-cut and doesn't drink and refers to God as a woman, whose formative development I can track online. But then I think about all the work I've already done with Eric. I think of our correspondence, the fevered, early-morning confessionals we indulged without shame. So when he calls at midnight and says, "I'm not a violent man," it doesn't matter if it's true. And when he says, "I know you are a person," and then hangs up, it doesn't matter that the words are slurred. What matters is that there is a record, of a call, of a conversation, of a girl on the other end.

5

n the morning, there is a text from Eric. It says, *I'll be home in four days. and I have a surprise.* I don't text him back because just as I'm sitting up in bed and noting the film on my teeth, I hear the unmistakable sound of someone doing Tae Bo downstairs and remember where I am. I remember Rebecca asking me to return her husband, and now that I have slept more than four hours, I feel less inclined to honor this request.

Just as my mother might crank Brooklyn Tabernacle Choir on Friday nights when my sole purpose was to sterilize the bathroom, Rebecca is another passive-aggressive alarm clock, her obedient clapping along to Billy Blanks a signal that it is no longer acceptable to sleep. But for once I've slept enough; I am delighted my body is still capable of issuing its own dopamine. Then I see my wilted sneakers in the corner and remember that I should be embarrassed. I try to find something wrong with the place, but I look around and it is pristine. Not beautiful, but carefully considered. On my bedside table, there is a bar of soap in the shape of a rose, a new toothbrush, sweatpants, and a T-shirt that says *Hudson Valley Tulip Festival*. I take a moment to pretend the room is mine. I press my face into the memory foam, and when I come up for air, Akila is standing in the doorway. Us being kinfolk notwithstanding, it is hard for me to empathize with a child whose footsteps are nearly undetectable. I did not even hear her open the door. Like her mother's, her silence is aggressive in its ease, and even though I usually have a hard time interacting with people's children, her shamelessness emboldens me, and I take a moment to really look at her, her shiny brown cheeks, her soft frown and Adventure Time nightshirt, her towering hair and balled fists. Because once upon a time my weird adolescent breasts were subject to the dissection of aunties everywhere, my BMI always a hot topic among the Jamaican deaconesses in our SDA church, I would like to mind my business when it comes to the subject of Akila's hair. However, it is a massive, two-foot condemnation of her limp-haired parents, who had clearly made some previous effort that did not pan out.

"You're the girlfriend," she says with no ire or judgment, which somehow makes it worse. I want to get out of bed, but sometime during the night I shed all my clothes. My underwear is on the floor between us, inside out. I am the adult here. I have bills. I am not slavering under the weight of my pituitary gland. But to demand that she respect me is so ludicrous that I can't get the words out of my mouth.

"Yeah," I say, and she frowns and shuts my door. In the

shower, the water pressure is excellent. I feel an unexpected reverence for my new toiletries. I use the soap but try not to smooth any of the dimples that constitute the petals. I use the toothbrush and relish the stiff bristles, the gross baking soda notes of their geriatric toothpaste, which is an appropriate departure from the sweet Peppa Pig brand I prefer. I can't remember the last time I brushed my teeth, and so, in this moment, I feel like a responsible person. I put on the sweatpants and T-shirt Rebecca laid out for me and decide that the only way I can repay her charity or leave this place with any semblance of dignity is to touch nothing and be as scarce as possible.

I restore the room to its original form and listen to the suburban quiet, the soft hybrid hum, the monastic baying of land-protecting dogs, the laughter of clear-skinned kids, a chorus of perpetually unlatched screen doors, and all the bugs, trying in earnest to fuck before they die. The calm is killing my peristalsis, but more pressing is my access to the Wi-Fi, so I go downstairs and Rebecca is there doing push-ups. She glances at me but doesn't say anything, and in fact seems to be angry, though maybe that's just what she looks like when she works out. I stand there in hopes that she might give me an opening, but the intensity of her focus is so keen, so uncomfortable to watch, that I retreat to the kitchen, where Akila is eating a bowl of cornflakes. She ignores me and I try to ignore her, but I don't know where they keep the cups.

"Where do you keep the cups?" I ask, in a small voice that surprises me. Akila sighs and slogs to the cabinet, reaches past all the normal glasses for a mug with a faded Captain Planet logo. I rinse it out, fiddle with a long-armed contraption attached to the tap, and fill the cup to the brim. I would like to forget our earlier interaction, but something about her general tween ennui won't let me shake that these years I have over her are mostly fraudulent and that I've seen her father's penis. However, I am so stunned by the clarity of the water that I briefly forget she is there while I go for seconds and thirds. When I ask for the Wi-Fi password, she points to the fridge. Between pictures of Eric in Greece and Akila in a sunflower costume is a note that says *deeppurple*. I type it into my phone and look at the picture of Akila again, the long yellow petals around her small, miserable face. I notice Akila is wearing a Superman tee.

"You like Superman?" I say, in that terrible small voice. "I like Superman."

"No one *likes* Superman," she says with an exasperated disdain that somehow brightens her face. Thankfully, Rebecca sweeps into the kitchen cradling what I assume is the family cat. It jumps out of her arms and darts through a doggy door, and aside from my awe that this round tabby is an outside cat, I feel a pang of recognition to find that this is the cat I saw during that first night, curled around Eric's leg.

"Fine, go," Rebecca says, opening the freezer, leaning inside. It makes me think of my own mother during the first years we lived in Latham, the way she was always too warm. The way a foot of snow would fall and glaze under freezing rain, and she would take the car and do doughnuts in the Walmart parking lot. Even sober, she was always sweating and keen on activities that made it worse, QVC tapes for capoeira, judo, and diaphragmatic circles. Rebecca withdraws from the freezer, guzzles a quart of water, and picks up the box of cornflakes.

"Make sure you go for a run today. At least a mile, okay?" she says as Akila slinks out of the room. Rebecca grabs a yogurt, looks at me, and then exits without another word. Back up in the guest room I plug the Wi-Fi password into my laptop and apply for more jobs. I open my perimeter, apply for a proofreading position at a gun magazine in Staten Island, a secretarial position at a clown school in Jersey City.

I go back down to the kitchen and Rebecca is putting on her shoes. When she sees me, she startles, then quickly regains herself. She tells me she is going out for groceries, and that feels odd. There is no reason I should know where she goes, but it is one of the more unfortunate results of our cohabitation. I already feel the pressure to overinform, to promise her that I am looking for work, and now, to make some sort of noise before I enter a room. I can tell she feels it, too, the absurdity of having to be accountable to me. She takes a moment to show me where they keep the bottled water and vitamins. As she does this, it almost feels as if she is angry with me. She opens the pantry, says, *if you need*, and throws the door closed. When she is gone, I walk around the house and familiarize myself. I find the light switches and take some time getting to know the sleek, high-tech kitchen and all its smooth, blinking dials. I can't seem to get used to the feel of carpet, and in each room I am always aware of it between my toes. As I am looking through the cookbooks, Akila comes in from a run. She does not acknowledge me. She takes a soda from the fridge, checks the calories, and puts it back.

"How was your run?"

"I don't know. Weird."

"Weird?" I say, and she picks up an apple, considers it for a while.

"People stare at me. When I go outside."

"What do you mean?"

"I mean, sometimes when I'm running or riding my bike, and I'll turn around and see one of the neighbors watching me."

"You should tell your parents," I say, and she puts down the apple, gives me a hard look.

"No. I don't want them to think— I've only been here for two years."

"This is your home."

"Yeah, well, I had three homes before this one," she says, which seems impossible. She seems too young.

"How old are you?"

"Twelve. Basically thirteen. And you're like, twenty-two?"

"Twenty-three."

"And you don't have your own place?"

"No, not anymore," I say, and her face softens.

"You should have a backup plan."

"What do you mean?"

"You know, for when this thing with my dad ends."

I go out to get some fresh air and try not to think about what Akila said. The neighborhood is fragrant and alien, all the hamlets in Maplewood bracketed in soft, emerald grass. Every half mile, there seems to be a golf course, with some improbable fauna, cranes and hare, circling little white carts along the fairways. There is a brief sunshower that curls my hair. A bird that is not a pigeon. An old white woman watching me through a slit in her blinds. I check my bank account, and my automatic student loan withdrawal has left me with thirty dollars. I leave a note on the fridge and hop on the bus and walk around Irvington, where my map shows the most demand. By demand, I mean maybe two delivery requests come in per hour. There is no bike share, so I have to go by foot. Then, halfway through my first delivery, the customer cancels.

A large order of pierogi comes in behind it. This is a relief, but when I arrive at the restaurant, the owner tells me a joke while I'm looking for the prepaid card and is insulted when I don't laugh. After this, no amount of friendliness can remedy what I've done, and she keeps making heavily accented remarks about "the app," which I think is a general screed about millennials, until she points at me and says, *Obama*, which is not by itself cause for alarm, but cause for me to look around the place, note all the ruddy Eastern European men, and want to get out of there. Pierogi in tow, I jog the two miles to my destination and find that the driveway itself is another half mile long. When my customer comes to the door, he extends his hand, and it is so soft as to be almost textureless. I realize he is Dr. Havermans, Park Slope's preeminent dermatologist, whose lo-fi ads have papered R, Q, and M trains since 1995. He is shorter in real life, with dark rings around his eyes, but I've never met a famous person before and when he asks if I want to come inside of course my answer is yes. He gives me three hundred dollars and asks me to take off my shoes, and I pocket the money and do what I have to do. And what I have to do is crush tomatoes and raw eggs with my feet while he listens to Arvo Pärt. He sends me on my way with a seaweed face cream, and in the grand scheme of things this is not even close to the worst thing I've done for money, but it makes me feel out of sorts all the same.

I take the train to my storage locker and grab a couple of paintbrushes, an osmotic suppository, an assorted collection of old Forever 21 basics, and an old tube of cyan. On the trip back, it occurs to me that I might not be able to get inside the house. I wonder if it was presumptuous to leave a note, if I was meant to attend dinner and am now late. For most of my life, I have not had to tell anyone where I planned to be. I could walk the length of Broadway without a face. I could perish in a fire and have no one realize until a firefighter came across my teeth in the ash. I walk from the station, and when I get to the house, I stand on the porch and enjoy the dense, late August air. It feels strange that only three months earlier, Eric pointed out my comma splice. I knock on the door and when no one answers, I go ahead and just walk inside. I pass by Akila's room and she is sitting at her vanity, struggling to pull a comb through her hair.

"Start from the ends," I say, and she gets up and closes her door. I retreat to the guest room and extract an eggshell from my sock. I delete the delivery app, retrieve the cyan, and start laying the foundation for a self-portrait, but every time something is wrong. Rebecca materializes in the doorway wearing a robe, long in the neck and the legs and indivisible from the silk.

"That dog has been at it all day," she says softly, and it feels like she means to be speaking to someone else. The way she is inclined toward me, waiting for a response, is what you do when there is already an established conversation, one that is developed enough to be open-ended. I was more comfortable when she was ignoring me. When I thought she regretted inviting me to stay.

"I don't hear anything," I say, and she frowns.

"I need your help with something," she says, and I follow her down the hallway into their bedroom. I try to appear less acquainted than I am, but I know she is watching me. I feel the recognition open on my face, though the lights are low, and there is newspaper all over the floor. She gives me one end of a fitted sheet. "Would you believe I've been trying to do this for half an hour?" she says, and no, I don't believe her. I look down at their bed and I think about them together, and it is not terrible because I want him to myself, but because all my thoughts of them in bed are mundane, of the late-night TV and morning breath and the sleepy, automatic spoon. After an initial struggle, we synchronize and decide the best course of action is to stuff the mattress upward into the sheet.

"You haven't told him I'm here," I say, and she lies down in the middle of the bed, spreads her arms and legs like a starfish.

"It hasn't really come up."

The next morning Eric texts me, *three days. not even going to guess what it is?* I don't respond because I would like to avoid the awkwardness of upstaging whatever the surprise actually is, and because the tenor of this question, his unsubtle displeasure at my lack of response, is a moment I want to savor. In my few years of dating, I have received a number of gifts from men. Gifts that were bought in haste at duty-free, that were fattening or detrimental to vaginal pH, that overestimated my interest in Lyndon B. Johnson and the New York Mets. I don't ever take it personally, but with Eric it's different. He knows what I used to do to my dolls. He knows that I let my second-grade crush pull three of my baby teeth. And so even if he gifted me airport whiskey, I would have to take it personally.

"I have an interview," I say to Rebecca after I get an email from the clown academy. I haven't prepared, but their "about us" page is informative and carefully laid-back, full of words like *moxie* and *disruption* and *Anakin, the office dog*. Rebecca is hunched over an orchid in the kitchen with a pair of silver shears. When she looks over at me I'm surprised to find she's wearing glasses.

"Is that what you're wearing?" she says, turning back to the orchid, the lenses of her glasses opaque with sun. She looks like a mad scientist, craned and tentative, the curved blades of the shears monstrous against the orchid's long, willowy stem.

"I just wanted you to know I'll be out of your hair soon," I say as she lops one of the bigger flowers off the stem.

"Goddamnit," she says, putting down the shears. "What are you talking to me about?"

"I have a job interview," I say, and now that she's looking directly at me, I know there's no reason I needed to share this with her, even though, weirdly, I was hoping she would be excited, that she would see how temporary this is and maybe never tell Eric I was here. Because there is no scenario in which telling him about this goes well. I have used her soap and left skin cells on her guest sheets, so it is maybe uncharitable to call Rebecca's hospitality a trap, and yet now we have a secret. Now I have also seen his wife and daughter in different stages of undress, screwed with the division of church and state, making any credible alternate reality impossible. To confess terrible things to each other online is easy, almost hypothetical. To be unemployed and wearing his wife's jeans is concrete. When the doorbell rings, Rebecca slips off her glasses and goes to answer the door. She returns with a boy who is holding a stack of books.

"This is Pradeep," she says, as he smoothes his polo, sits down at the kitchen table. She doesn't introduce us. She calls for Akila, once, twice. When Akila doesn't come down, Rebecca runs upstairs and leaves us alone together. He doesn't look at me. He sets down an iced coffee, opens up three dog-eared books, and arranges them in a row. I didn't like teenage boys even when I was a teenager myself, but I am desperate for him to like me, even as his belted khakis are bumming me out. He finishes his coffee and then extends the empty cup.

"Could you throw this out?" he says without looking at me, as Akila comes down the stairs wearing a wig, a green one this time. Rebecca is close on her heels looking wrung-out, but I notice that she has put on mascara and let down her hair.

"Sorry, Pradeep," she says, smiling with her teeth. I realize she is flirting, and it is so unsettling that I go back up to the guest room, where I try to calm my interview jitters by streaming *Mister Rogers' Neighborhood*. For a moment it works. In the neighborhood of make-believe King Friday is judging an art contest, but Lady Elaine Fairchilde will not submit to his judgment. She says art is subjective, and technically that is the moral of the story, though it is also implied that everyone in the kingdom thinks her art is bad, which—if she is making art that is meant to be seen by others—is a serious tough-titty, the comfort of audience subjectivity pretty much null when the audience is everyone, and everyone has decided, subjectively, that the art is bad. Then Mister Rogers takes us into a crayon factory, and when two disembodied hands pour yellow wax into a trough filled with holes and the piano accompaniment comes in, it is just too much. I pause it and find the Wikipedia for Pomeranian, so that I can go into my interview with talking points about the office dog, who is, per Wikipedia, one of an extremely horny breed. The guest room is hotter than the other rooms, and so I head downstairs to gather myself, but while I'm on the stairs I hear Pradeep say, *a monkey could do this*, and all I can see is the back of Akila's head, the halo of green, synthetic frizz.

"I'm trying," she says, a tremor in her voice.

"You're not. It's simple math," he says, and I go down there and start looking for the Captain Planet mug, though it is just an excuse to linger. I glance at Akila and she looks upset, though I can sense that my looking at her makes it worse.

"Hey," I say, turning to Pradeep, my small voice back again. "You can't—"

"Can you not?" Akila says, and so I don't. I grab my things and take a bus to Jersey City, where I find that the clown academy is housed in a squat, neoclassical building that, compared with the bagel shops and degraded coworking spaces along the block, appears eerie and slightly outside of time. Inside, it is like a chapel, replete with modern fresco, the imagery familiar only in its rippled triceps and biblical postures, because upon closer inspection every figure depicted is a clown. Above the receptionist's desk there is an engraving that says, *The clown stands on his head and sees the world the right way up.* The receptionist is an impossibly chic Asian woman with long, tattooed hands and some sort of head cold. Naturally it heartens me to see some color in the place, but when she escorts me to the waiting room she sneezes and tells me that I'm underdressed. This is an understatement. Per my cursory scan of the company mission statement, the ball pit, break room Ping-Pong, and office dog, I thought the office dress would be casual. But when I step into the room, there are five other applicants combing furiously through their notes. They are all wearing pantsuits and they are all Asian. I sit down and pull the school's website up on my phone. When the interviewer calls my name, his eyes sweep over me with confused disinterest and it is humiliating, but I feel a vague racial obligation to see it through. So I sit down and immediately there is a mutual feeling of us just going through the motions, though the interviewer, a white man decked out in Tommy Bahama who tells me to address him as Maestro, gives me a rundown of the school beginning with an extremely defensive condemnation of the Ringling Brothers and magic of the lowest common denominator, which includes the decorative—cards and spitting flowers and buzzers—but not, he stresses, the intricate art of tying balloons. This interview seems to be mostly about him getting things off his chest, which is fine because I'm clearly not the front-runner for this job, and the more he talks about the historic model of the Italian buffoon, the more I realize I have misunderstood the requirements of the job. For a brief moment I think that the format of this interview is itself a joke and the successful applicant is meant to call the bluff, but then he goes on a tear about glove puppets and the mime's blatant appropriation of indigenous clown rituals, and I just feel disappointed in myself for needing this job so desperately and for being as black as I am and for coming unprepared.

He tells me that he's firing the current receptionist because she is too whimsical with visitors, and I tell him that I thought clowning was supposed to be fun. He leans back in his chair and closes his eyes, which seems a very dramatic response to an extremely unsurprising observation. In the protracted silence, I notice that Anakin the Pomeranian is sitting stoically in the corner, apparently not horny at all. Then Maestro leans forward and places a clown nose on the desk. He asks me to look at it. He asks me if I feel like laughing. When I tell him I don't he smiles and says that's because clowning is about interrogating the human condition, that it is art, and that these are serious things. He tells me that the art that matters is the art that is wrought and consumed with great difficulty. He tells me a laugh is easy, and when there is a prioritization of fun, clowning ceases to be art and becomes entertainment. Then he gives me a grave, buzzerless handshake and tells me my time is up. On the bus back, I keep thinking about the nose. About how strange it looked out of context. I don't mind his condescension, and I can't remember the last time I laughed.

When I get to the house it is dark. Rebecca is doing yoga in the living room to a muted video, and I am primed to go feel more nothing in my room, but I see the sofa and find it more attractive than the stairs. I splay on the sofa and watch her, her taut ta-dasana and uttanasana, and her unimpeachable plank. She is efficient but imperfect, seamless but still apparently holding the form in the front of her mind, the effort to arch her feet and com-press her abdominal muscles propelling her out of her pose. She trembles through a half moon, collapses, and shimmers on the mat. She glances at me, but doesn't ask me to leave. When she continues on into her next pose, I realize I hoped she would. It reminds me of how she undressed in the morgue, and I envy the nonchalance she has about her body.

It is not a perfect body, and in fact mine is better, though hers is smaller by a size or two. I feel boring for the compulsion to com-pare myself to her, and even a little mean, but her serenity both-ers me. It bothers me that she doesn't wear prettier underwear, that her marriage is inscrutable and involved, and that I am somewhere inside it. I get onto my knees and join her on the carpet, and even this small action is enough to render my body into a font of unsavory noise. Rebecca makes room but does not look at me. We enter corpse pose, and as we lie side by side, I hear her short, irregular breaths and understand the degree of her effort. It feels personal. The finite oxygen, the smell of yeast and salt, deodorant and shampoo, the body when it is most conspicuously an organism, a thing that can weep and degrade. I rise with her into something called dolphin pose, and it feels silly until it burns. I used to exercise with my mother. A new diet guide or juicing blade would arrive in the mail, and for a week we would eat only cabbage soup. For a week we would attempt a kosher Atkins, my mother emerging from the Seventh-day Adventist pantry with steak substitutes made of plant protein. We bought in bulk but always seemed to eat very little, one week just coffee with Danish butter, the next week only foods that were yellow or green. While my father took women into his study, we descended upon the living room in Lycra for Zumba, eight-minute abs, or whatever lo-fi glute blasting was available via early aughts on-demand, alternating between tearful, formerly fat barre gurus, white capitalist body-posi rah-rahs with creepy yonic overtones, and the more classic motivational speakers who slap you over the face with a box of Ho Hos and compel you to squat. We were bonded in our mutual hatred of our bodies, though my hatred was adolescent and hers was infinitely more developed, partly a trick of her newly sober brain, which found in food a substitute for the narcotics that had kept her lean. By the time she killed herself, she would still be eleven pounds shy of her goal.

After another measure in corpse, I follow Rebecca into the kitchen and watch her portion ingredients. She pushes a clove of garlic in front of me and offers me a knife, blade first. When I take the knife, a thought comes to me fully rendered, complete with texture and aftermath: I could, in the right state of mind, murder her and carry on with my life. Really it would be her fault, for inviting a stranger into her house and providing the knife. Her composure is infuriating. I start to tell her that when I fuck her husband, I'm the one who does the fucking. But the impulse passes, and I spoon the garlic into the oil. The sirloin follows, and as the potatoes are coming out of the oven, one of Rebecca's big oven mitts slips off and onto the floor. She sucks the burned finger and then forgets about it to take a bite of the steak. She offers me her fork and I follow suit, the meat bloody and tough. It is the best thing I have eaten in weeks. I close my eyes. When I open them, she is smiling.

"How long have you known Pradeep?" I say, and she tilts her head.

"I don't know. A few years. He's a good kid," she says, *good kid* a little gooier than the rest of the words.

"You like him."

"He's young. He hasn't been disappointed yet. Sometimes I forget what that looks like—you know, optimism," she says, and I want to ask how old she is, but I refrain. "Why do you ask?"

"It just seemed like he was being kind of hard on her."

"She needs a firm hand," she says, though she has stopped eating, stopped smiling.

"It wasn't like that. The way he was talking to her, it felt— specific," I say, and there is no fluffy alternative word for what I'm trying to convey, no way to effectively explain violations that are not overt. It is a rhetorical hellscape. A casual reduction so frequent it is mundane. Almost too mundane for the deployment of the R word, as with a certain sect of Good White Person the accusation overshadows the act. *Racism!* I should yell, because I'm sure Rebecca will receive it in the uppercase regardless, and already I feel her seizing on the drama of its implication, even though racism is often so mundane it leaves your head spinning, the hand of the ordinary in your slow, psychic death so sly and absurd you begin to distrust your own eyes. So it has taken a long time for me to get here. To say, *Yes, this is what happened. It happened just like that.* But when Rebecca turns and scrapes the rest of her food off the plate and into the trash, I feel like a jerk. She looks at me, any goodwill that existed between us lost.

"I am her mother," she says firmly, though there is a hitch in her voice and her face colors. "You are a guest," she says before she sweeps out of the room, and I find it very rich, to have been invited here partly on the absurd presumption that I would know what to do with Akila simply because we are both black, and now be rebuffed when I have not performed the role of the Trusty Black Spirit Guide to her taste. I go back up to the guest room and pack my things. I wait for her to put me out. I lie in the dark with my shoes on, wondering if I was wrong to say anything. I compile everything I could have said if I were faster, smarter. By midnight, I have a carefully footnoted Spike Lee joint, an entire treatise on the conspiracy of oppression, though at one o'clock when I have rehearsed my supporting data and reimagined our conversation as one in which I don't let Dr. King down, I suddenly feel that she can go fuck herself, that my intellectual labor should be subsidized and the onus is not on the oppressed to consider the oppressor, though in the morning after I take a shower, I look out of the window and see her lugging a bag of mulch across the yard and I feel guilty all over again. Her chunky, tragic sneakers and freaky competence. The way the windows around the cul-de-sac are dark and she is the only person outside, already engaged enough in her task to be making a lot of supremely unsexy noise. It becomes clear to me, how keenly she is alone.

I creep around the house and try to be racially neutral. I avoid her as best I can, though I hear her all around the house: doing dishes, Pilates, and some involved activity with a power drill. In my effort to be sensitive to where she is, I find that she is an extremely noisy person. I can't say whether this is for my benefit, but even on the other side of the house the noise feels indirectly violent, her predilection for walking on her heels and shouting *yes!* to her *Insanity* DVD well within the realm of plausible deniability, but intimidating nonetheless. So I keep mostly to the guest room and scan through jobs. I look at availabilities in the city, but even if I was granted an interview, I have no idea where I'd be commuting from. I browse StreetEasy, and every neighborhood in my price range is lousy with sexual predators. Just as an experiment, I see what comes up if I keep my search within Jersey. I check the commute from the house to a small textbook publisher in Hoboken, and it is a straight shot. I imagine what it might be like to ride exclusively on NJ Transit, which has significantly less feces than the G. I read through requirements for entry-level jobs that are not requirements so much as requests that the applicant have "a good sense of humor" and basic tech literacy for 41K a year. I tweak my résumé, omit *coordinator* from my title, and revise my role as more author-facing. I stress my editorial involvement, though the author of the Flounder series stopped calling me when I made him a mixtape.

I pull up our email chain and find the mixtape. I sent it at 1:43 a.m., after the author wrote to tell me that squid have doughnut-shaped brains. I look at the track list and wonder where I went wrong. *The esophagus passes through a central hole in the brain. If they overeat, they risk brain damage.* I wonder if I was too earnest, if I relied too heavily on Mazzy Star. I stop applying for jobs and look for a reputable camgirl site, though I have some trouble linking my PayPal and the traffic is low. I sit in front of the camera in my bra for half an hour and only get one patron. Mostly he just reads the paper, but then he folds it up and sends a message through the chat that says *kill yourself, nigger bitch.* I log off and think about the clown nose. I look outside and Akila and Rebecca are in the garden wearing wide-brimmed hats. They are kneeling in front of a single tomato, and for a moment, they look completely alike, the plant the center of their silent communion. Then Akila takes off a glove and cradles the tomato in the palm of her hand. They turn to each other and laugh. I try to figure out what was funny, but I can't, so I go to the master bathroom and look through the cabinets, and inside

everything is generic and mostly expired except for the narcotics. I take two Percocet and save a fentanyl patch for later. The
bottles all bear Rebecca's name, though the triazolam is the only
one with her middle name, which turns out to be *Moon*. Underneath the sink, there is an old-school douche bag that is warm to
the touch. There is a modest purple vibrator with three speeds,
cotton balls, hydrogen peroxide, hair dye, and black nail polish.
I take the nail polish. I can't imagine her painting her nails, but
I can imagine her on the bathroom tile, prepping the douche
with Vaseline. When I imagine it, she is indifferent, her vagina
defying all etymology, not a pussy or a twat but an abstract violence, like a Rorschach or a xenomorph. For me, I've had little
choice. The moment I left Clay's house, my vagina was a cunt.

I go to the window and make sure they're still out in the garden.
I take a few pictures of them and delete the ones with too much
sun. I do a sweep under the bed. There are board games and
unopened bags of soft, red clay. There is a battered version of
Sorry, a Boggle with a cracked dome, and a sleek chessboard
with a compartment for pieces. Inside, there are two queens and
a pouch of tulip seeds. It seems strange that these would be kept
under the bed, strange that they would have board games at
all. Everything is too ordinary, too sweet. I can't imagine Rebecca suspending her disbelief long enough to move a piece, I
can't imagine Akila tolerating the cheer of her father, and yet
there they are outside in the garden, laughing with each other.
My mother was not a woman who laughed. She didn't laugh
because (1) she could see that everyone who heard it was

unpleasantly surprised and (2) after we moved upstate, nothing was funny. She told stories about the home economics courses they offered in rehab, about how they gave her a succulent shaped like a hand and taught her a different way to pack a suitcase. These stories were not humorless. She smiled when she talked about the holding cell in Harlem, about the plainclothes police officers who sat outside her apartment in unmarked cars. She told me that cowboys could be women, could be black. She watched multicamera sitcoms exclusively, left the TV on low during the night so that my dreams became elastic and improvisational, primed to make sense of the canned laughter always in the air. She was disappointed to find I had inherited her ugly, glottal laugh, and encouraged me to hold it behind my hand.

We went to church and clapped softly to an instrumental of "He Lives." We wore plain, shapeless clothes and washed each other's feet. At a more relaxed, secular church a mile down the road, the pastor gave the sermon from his drum kit. In our church, my mother tried to befriend scared vegetarian women who smelled the city and turned their heads. The sun went down and the TV turned on. We went to Waldenbooks and my mother bought my weekly sketchbook. She stood in Self-Help with her hand in her hair. At home, she put on "Dancing Queen" over the TV. Underneath ABBA, Suzanne Somers emerged from the shower as John Ritter placated the landlord with his floppy wrists. My mother danced and waxed poetic about 1977, the year she was seventeen. She lay on the floor and said, *It's all boring when I'm not high*, the ceiling fan turning in her eyes.

———————

When I put the chessboard back, I notice another game a little farther back, underneath a pair of dirty gingham shorts. When I bring it out, I see immediately that it is Monopoly, which was my father's favorite game. It was his favorite game because he always won, and he always won because he always played against me. He believed in the purity of competition. He did not believe that a child deserved to win simply for being a child. He scooped up my properties and smiled, showed the gold fillings in his teeth. Once, I tucked a few blue dollars into my dollhouse in the middle of the night. Now I look for my father's favorite piece, the boot. But the game and the pieces are missing, and in their place is a Glock 19. This was one of Clay's favorites. He owned three, and in his apartment, one was always nearby. When he held it, he held it casually. When I take the gun into my hands now, it does not feel casual. The gun itself is ugly. It is heavy and inelegant, but in my hand, I see how it is lethal, ingenious technology. Rebecca texts me from outside and says that she and Akila are going out for back-to-school supplies, and it occurs to me that it is September. I stand at the window, and I watch them drive away. I consider the gun and notice I have an incoming call.

"Eric," I say, embarrassed by the apparent relief in my voice.

"She lives," he says, and I sense his irritation. It should make me happy, but his anger is different when it is not theoretical, and I panic.

"I'm so sorry."

"I thought you were dead."

"You did?"

"Of course not. But I worried. I worry about you in that neighborhood."

"You worry about me?" I say, because I like the idea of someone out there wondering if I've died, though in the moment his whiteness is unbearable. Also I know he is just trying to make me feel bad about not responding, but even this performative concern feels good. "It's just Bushwick."

"Have you looked at the crime map? They update it regularly. A good amount of forced sodomy in your area. Rebecca got mugged coming out of the supermarket eight years ago. Two miles away from our house. Guy took her ring and I had to get her a new one."

"How's the conference going?"

"It's good. All these NARA nerds. I feel at home. But I miss you."

"I don't believe you," I say, putting him on speakerphone so I can hold the gun.

"No, I do. I mean that. I've had a lot of time to think up here. You know when you go to a hotel and get one of those rough towels, and the toilet is sealed and certified with a sticker? That's Toronto. Clean. Everyone has great skin."

"What have you been thinking about?" I ask, because I've never been to a hotel.

"A lot of things. I was working with some glass plate negatives. T. E. Lawrence. The negatives were so degraded I went back to the hotel and found flakes of the film inside my glove. I put them under a light and mostly it was a wash, but in one or two I could still see the desert, the color-reversed sand. And I just felt like, fuck, this exact thing is happening to me, you know, cellularly." He laughs, and I can tell he is embarrassed. For a moment, I think I love him. I hold the gun with two hands.

"I totally get that."

"I could leave my wife," he says.

"What?"

"I could leave her. Easily."

"Okay."

"Listen, I have to go now but I'll be home in three days. Let's talk about it then?" He hangs up, and for a while I just sit there with the gun in my lap. I open my photo gallery and look at the picture of Rebecca and Akila in the garden. I put the gun back in the box, push it back under the bed, and wander around the house. I imagine all of it is mine. But even when I make myself comfortable, when I find an orange and eat it over the sink, I have the sensation of stepping into someone else's shoes. I know that if Eric leaves his wife, we'll have to move to another town. A suburb with rival high schools. A small apartment stocked with wax paper and bananas. A lightly used American car that we share. A place where our shoes appear side by side. A cabinet full of plastic Price Chopper bags and a nervous old dog that loves him more than it loves me. I could do it, though as I press the rind into the trash and see all the proof of life, the soggy cornflakes and chicken fat, I know that his declaration, the dangling carrot for which mistresses everywhere open their stupid mouths, is complete bullshit. Believing he will leave Rebecca is one of the few personal failures I can absolutely avoid, but then I see that picture of him in Greece again, his pit stains and passport necklace and vacation stubble, and I just eat it up. Because I have not been laid in a month, and everything looks good. Men in magazines who wear chambray and pretend to water plants. That self-portrait of Rembrandt where his collar is turned up. The Allstate insurance man and Stringer Bell. Thirty days have passed since Eric and I last fucked, and it is agony. I take the picture off the fridge and head to my room, but on the way I notice the door to Akila's room is open.

Inside it smells like body butter and Hot Pockets, like a rank, pubescent Yankee Candle, but otherwise, this is the most fantastic room in the house. The cutesy *stay out* sign on the door now seems out of step if not ironic, the room less the product of petulant stoicism and more a tribute to earnest fandom, the walls papered in dragons, wiccan infographics, and lithe Korean boys, quartz and drusy stones and dirty zirconia hanging from strategically placed tacks, Gothic illustrations of woodland faeries on linen, steampunk goggles strapped to a wig stand where seven wigs are stacked in accordance with ROYGBIV. On the TV there are several figurines, though the only ones I recognize are Robin and the Takashi Murakami miniature of a girl spraying milk from her tits. Because of my sexless career as a high school studio art kid, I was frequently adjacent to the prototypes for girls like this, girls who were horse-girls except with cats, girls with patches and pins who uploaded their Suicide Girl auditions with the translucent computer lab Macs, girls who were Goth-lite, in and out of Hot Topic and Torrid with their weepy, sallow boys, shy dabblers in anime and D&D, though in the years I have been away I see it has gotten sexier and more bleak, the interludes between Akila's shrines to Guillermo del Toro and Tim Burton dripping in intermediate sorcery and sex, bloody grindhouse stills framed next to fishnets and a wilted go-go boot, all the hairless CGI men with their hips canted, corollaries of the comic stacks and spell scrolls and everything else exalting the perfect and unreal.

Weirdly, the frankness of this intensity is hard on my conscience. I look through her closet and feel terrible about it. I find a cache of notebooks and scan through them, and all of it is raw—cruel, longing portraits of her classmates, careful records of calorie allotments, and in one totally nondescript composition notebook, pages upon pages of Batman fan fiction. I read it for a while because it is pretty good. The characters are believably drawn, Bruce Wayne out and about in Gotham in his playboy iteration, attending an auction for the last model of the gun that killed his parents, losing the auction to a black, omniscient sprite that is clearly Akila's surrogate, though Clark Kent becomes more prominent as the story goes on, lounging around the Batcave post breakup with Lois Lane, who doesn't take him seriously as a journalist or a man. I do not expect this fan fiction to become about how he reclaims his manhood, and I do not expect the lengthy description of the soaps in Bruce's bat-shaped bath. Here, there are some character problems, the exclamation points in Batman's dialogue ultimately less believable than his sexual awe and jealousy, as he is a human man with a complicated belt and Clark is an intergalactic softboi with infinite strength. It's so dirty and engrossing that I don't notice Akila until she is ripping the notebook out of my hands. She clutches it against her chest and looks at the floor. To see her there, the embarrassment open on her small face, feels like seeing an Olive Garden commercial after having already plowed through two bowls of fettuccini. The stark photorealism always beyond a terrible indulgence, in this case the invasion of her privacy, which I had shrugged off as an extension of Rebecca's, though of course that was incorrect. Once Akila herself is grounded in the context of her room, her vulnerability, her personhood, is concrete. She doesn't speak and puts the notebooks exactly where they were. It is strange to see that even these secret things have a fixed place. If I destroyed this marriage, I would be destroying this, too.

"Can you please leave?" she says in a high voice, her back still turned. I leave and go outside and have a cigarette. I am a creep. My bowels don't work and maybe there are other things inside me that are dead, but there is so much life around me, tomatoes that beat the bugs and rot, waiting to be held by a hand. I watch the sunset. I'm not sure what day it is. Technically early September is not fall, but so many of the trees are already bald. Across the way that same white lady is watching me through her blinds. I salute her and she recedes. Rebecca comes out and glances at me, fishing her keys from her purse.

"A body came in. I have to work," she says, and though she is speaking to me, I feel our last conversation still in the air. Her eyes linger on my cigarette and I think she's going to ask me to put it out, but instead she asks for one. I light her up. "Akila has tae kwon do in an hour," she says, turning to unlock her car. "You can take the Volvo. The studio is a mile down the road, in the shopping center." She gets into her Lincoln Navigator and tears out of the driveway, and inside Akila is already dressed in her gi.

Later, we proceed to the car. She puts her gear in the back and we slide silently into our seats. It is only once I'm behind the wheel that I realize this is Eric's car. I start the engine and try not to think about the last time I was in this spot, in his lap, the memory of his fist a heat behind my eyes. I open the glove compartment, and there are a handful of watermelon Jolly Ranchers. There is also a flask, and I close it quickly, glance at Akila to see if she saw. But she is looking out of the window, already engaged in the merciful act of pretending I'm not here. I haven't driven in three years. I pull out onto the road and stop short at a red light. I turn and look at Akila, and beyond her there is an actual deer. I roll down the window and yell at it because I'm already dealing with too many moving parts. Akila turns and glares at me, and then her face softens and grows nervous. I know it's because she can tell I'm nervous, and that makes it worse.

"Do you know how to drive?"

"Yes," I say, though when it starts to rain I scramble to find the switch for the wipers. She reaches over calmly and switches them on. I hunch over the wheel and continue on. After a harrowing seven minutes, we arrive at the shopping center. The dojang is sitting between a dimly lit Morton Williams and a nail parlor that has begun to scroll down its metal door. She takes her bag and goes inside. I park the car and for a while I go back and forth on whether it would be weirder to stay in the car or go in. Eventually I go inside because I need to use the bathroom. After, I take a seat behind a group of ornery parents who occasionally look up from their phones to clap. The practice is so structured, it is almost nonviolent, the master a stocky, terrifying man who circles the mat as they run through leg extensions and isolated abdominal work, endurance drills that they count off in Korean in increments of ten, a few adults in the mix who are being very dramatic during the stretching portion, everyone doing assisted butterflies and half splits and almost certainly farting up a storm. The dojang smells like it was scooped out of someone's belly button, but after fifteen minutes I don't smell anything but Lysol and the seasoned plastic of used sparring gear. There are co-instructors wandering around, and for the most part they are cheerful and nondescript, but one of them is black and when I catch his eye, he pauses in the middle of his form and smiles. Like most hyper-symmetrical black men, his smile is a disarming show of contrasts and, in this case, anchored by an obscene pair of dimples. I smile back at him and think bitterly about my abstinence. His eyes are bright and kind, and so of course I picture our children, our rent, and our amicable divorce in the time it takes him to move along as the students run around the mat in bare feet, count through axe and crescent kicks and land light blows on each other as the master grunts his approval of the more crisp performers and attends to the stereo, which, underneath the agony of the class, is playing the soundtrack from *The Matrix Reloaded.*

Akila is in the middle of it, hitting her marks with confidence and even a little style, her place in the hierarchy clear even without the signifier of her belt, a dark purple that I see on only one other student. Her focus is so intense it is almost embarrassing to watch, though when they bring out a stack of small pine boards for breaking drills and I see her go through three at once my breath catches in my throat. Then the master takes the other purple belt, a small white girl with dark, sunken eyes, and the class settles down onto their knees as she and Akila spar. It is over quickly. Aside from a brief fall onto her back, Akila is reserved, less interested in force and more invested in precision, her contact so light and matter-of-fact you can feel her keeping careful score, an infuriating thing for her partner, who is good, but too upset by Akila's composure to compete.

"That pairing seems a little unfair. Look at her," a parent says. Of course, it is not unfair. They are of the same belt and roughly the same age. Akila extends her hand, and the girl turns her back. In the car, Akila guzzles a bottle of water and takes out her phone to record the calories burned.

"You were amazing," I say, but Akila just turns the radio up. I'm excited to hear that it is Sister Sledge.

"I hate this," she says, connecting her phone to the aux cord, putting on what sounds like Japanese ska. We travel in silence. I glance at her and again she is turned to the window. She seems smaller now, more the girl who held the notebook to her chest. The song turns out to be over six minutes long and relentlessly manic, the trumpet and gurgling bass alternating over rapid-fire Japanese.

"I thought it was good," I say as we pull into the driveway.

"What?" she says, already halfway out of the car.

"Your story," I say, and she stops and looks back at me, her eyes soft. Then she turns, shoulders her gear, and marches into the house without another word. Rebecca is still not home, and so when I look through the pantry, I take my time. I find a box of powdered milk and take it to my room. I mix it with some water in my Captain Planet mug and then I add a little of the cyan. I find my palette and mix a few more shades of blue. I open my photo gallery and find the picture of Akila and Rebecca. I take a book from the living room and tear out the copyright page. I work until 3 a.m., until the two of them are down on the torn, yellowed paper, craned over a single tomato. In my sleep, Clark Kent arrives on the planet alone and falls into endless wealth, and across the country, a young Bruce Wayne is adopted by sweet, midwestern parents. There is no Batman, but there is still a Superman, a deadened Übermensch who imposes his idea of purity onto the earth.

In the morning, I wake up in a panic. It is not just that Eric will be home in a day and I still haven't found a way to leave or tell him I was here. It's that I've forgotten something. I wash up in the sink and throw on some clothes. Downstairs Rebecca is asleep on the couch in her jacket, and for a moment I pause and take her in, her open mouth and soft, nasal snore. On the train into the city I consider other men. All of them are asleep and exotic in their inertia, so still and distant that I'm free to notice their throats and fingernails. The train car is silent and filled with innocuous trash, a newspaper open to a group of charter school kids lobbing softballs in Ditmas Park, an umbrella stripped and inverted like an aluminum flower. The doors jam at every platform, but no one is coming in. During a long transfer, two Swedes roll by with teal suitcases, and a tired violinist leans away from the wall, props his violin under his chin, and then reconsiders.

I arrive at my old apartment and feel no tenderness toward it. The stairwell is still rotting and the roaches are still capable of flight. My landlord is there in what was presented in the apartment listing as a laundry room, but which is in actuality a room where 4C deals coke and where the walls are brimming with hardy city bees. I can hear the bees in the walls when I speak to her. I tell her that I left something behind of great sentimental value, and as I was not the best tenant, I am prepared to give her a light bribe, two five-dollar bills, but she pauses in the middle of whisking her matcha and says to go ahead. She says, *We should've partied more*, and smiles, revealing to me some new information, which is that I was at some point prominent enough in her world to party with, and that she is missing a tooth. I try to think of something to say as she sifts through a drawer of keys. I feel bad for how I avoided her every time rent was coming due, and I think about the hypothetical drugs we could've done together, what it would've been like to hold back her hair. She says, *It was a bummer to evict you*, and then I go upstairs and the place is freshly painted and spackled, the wet ecru making it feel for a moment like beyond the barred windows and brick there might be a sun. I close my eyes and enjoy the smell of the wet paint, the synthetic resin exact in where it shreds the sinuses. There is no sign I was ever here and that is kind of a relief. I reach into the back of my closet. If I'm honest, a part of me hopes the painting won't be there. But it is still there, and when I give the keys back to my landlord, I make sure the canvas is turned away. On the train, that isn't so easy. A few commuters look up from their phones and stare, and there is a man in a corner seat who keeps looking at my painting like he has never seen a dead woman before.

By the time I get back to the house, the afternoon is gone. Akila is shut up in her room with a K-drama and Rebecca is up and about, a moist yoga mat unfurled on the floor. She emerges from the bathroom with a roll of tinfoil, looks at my painting, and doesn't comment on it. She asks if I can help her dye her hair. As I begin to apply the dye, she adjusts the towel around her neck and glares at herself in the mirror with such a private disdain that I feel I shouldn't be in the room. Our eyes meet in the mirror and I hold her gaze, though sustained eye contact has a way of quickly becoming unfriendly, the ratty terry cloth cape and tinfoil mohawk a sympathetic combination on any other woman, but sort of scary on her. I tell her to get on her knees. I bend her over the tub and secure her by the neck. She presses her face into the towel and I rinse the dye out, and it is only then that I think about the color, the blond now black, making her look paler, a little dissonant, like an adult actress assuming the role of Snow White. She looks at herself in the mirror and smiles, disappears into her room and comes out in all black. She asks me if

I have any plans, though of course it is not really a question, and she ushers me outside, where there is an angry, orange dusk.

We get in the car and don't speak. She turns the radio to an AM channel where a sleepy voice is talking about submarine acoustics, describing in detail how sound waves carve through leagues of water and function as an eye. She lowers the windows and lets her hair down, and as we pull into a small twenty-four-hour garage, the stars are coming out. After she laces up her boots and presses three studs into the cartilage of her ear, which in descending order appear to be a heart, a fist, and a Star of David, we walk past an ammo depot and a half-lit school bus lot and cut through a shaggy line of trees, the woods truncated and swollen with rain, opening to a field with an elevated soundstage where three men emerge from underneath their hair. She offers me a cup of whiskey and downs her own with a determination that darkens her face, the crowd around us frothy and homogeneous, white men relieved by the idea that they deserve to be angry, though in their spit and lean you can see they are aware of their performance and so to close this gap of enviable trauma by god they better make it good, better get in the pit and extract some teeth.

Rebecca looks disappointed by the crowd. She turns to me and says that everyone is old. She says she doesn't know when it happened. She offers me a drink that looks like river water and says it's a martini. I take a sip and it does not taste great, the vermouth

and gin dominated entirely by a greasy residue I now realize has
come from the olives, which are stuffed with cheese. The paper
cup is already giving way. She removes her ring, slides it into her
pocket, and tells me not to make a big deal of it. She says not everything Means Something and in fact, a lot of things mean nothing, and technically this is the beauty of music that prioritizes
brawn. And by brawn, what she means is force. What she means
is speed. There is a curtain of mist around the stage. This is likely
due to lighting and a few discreetly placed smoke machines, but
as the lead guitarist indulges a brief aside about Helsinki's transit
system, I see the human component of the humidity, the carbon
dioxide and salivary thrust, the centrifuge of salt and hair.

As the next song starts, Rebecca says that she used to attend
these concerts mostly as a function of being someone's girlfriend. She was not permitted to have an opinion so much as
observe these boyfriends' exhibitions of taste, which for the particular sect of Hyde Park thrash-lite boys that Rebecca favored,
meant maintaining a steady supply of safety pins and gauze,
meant Elmer's glue and DIY tattoos with straight pins and india
ink, meant conversations in porta-potties about dragons and the
bourgeoisie, critiques on the augmentation of capital in the form
of pierced white boys from upstate New York, railing against
their parents and the banks and *society*, which was a word she
said so much it began to sound like it was a word they made up.
At fifteen Rebecca cleaned the blood out of her Docs and began
to feel like she did not actually care about capitalism, like she
did not care about authenticity, because at these concerts, which

were about the scourge of assimilation, there was somehow still a code of dress, and the only thing that made it good was the brawn, the punch she felt inside her ears, the entropy and crystallized core of communal violence that is impossible to contain. She rakes her hair out of her face and says that Eric was a welcome aberration. A guy who called soda *pop*, a guy who didn't like piercings, who listened unironically to the bedazzled canker that is disco. He seemed earnest, not like the rest of her boyfriends, who of course went on to work for the banks. I follow her gaze to the medical tent, where a man is being lowered onto a stretcher. She scoffs and orders another drink at the bar, and then we move into the crowd, where she bares her teeth and rips off her shirt. A man barrels toward us, takes the shirt, and disappears. She doesn't seem to mind. She drags me into the mosh, removes her bra, and tosses it toward the stage. I try to honor the spirit of the thing and not pay too much attention to her breasts, which are lovely and small and slightly mismatched. These are the sort of breasts you need if you want to mosh, and as the lead guitarist circles his finger and says *Grind!* Rebecca pulls me in deeper, leading with her cute, unmoving breasts, and everything is crunchy and in a minor key, two walls made of arms careening toward each other, the impact a compression I feel in my uterus, a man in an AARP shirt coming right for me and pulling me down by my hair and into the hard, brown grass, where there are cigarette butts and Band-Aids and crushed Dixie cups. As I claw my way up for air, I look around and realize I've lost her, though during my time on the ground someone stepped on the back of my neck with one of those four-pound platform Docs and I did not completely hate it, and though the music is bad—it is bad like a deviated septum, like acid reflux, like a monkey paw—damage is incurred for a necessary indulgence, which is to take a man by the ears and get him down and stomp on his open, consenting face, this glee cut a little short when I see Rebecca is just fine, near the front of the stage with mud caked between her tits. In this moment, maybe we are on the same page. But everything is temporary, and in an hour she buys a new shirt from the merch table, and we walk silently to the car, a chill in the air that reminds me that soon it will be fall.

"I let Pradeep go," she says once we're on the road. "I talked to Akila. I didn't know. I thought she just hated math." I look under my fingernails and every single one is caked with dirt. "Can I ask—what was it that you heard? What did he say to her?"

"He said, a monkey could do this."

"Jesus," she says softly. We travel for a while in silence, take the exit toward Maplewood. "That painting you had. What was that?"

"A portrait of my mother."

We get out of the car, and she shields her face as two headlights come into view. We turn to look as the taxi stops at the curb. I think of how we look, the mud on our faces, the grass in our hair, the crowdsourced blood on our clothes. She looks at me and smiles darkly, and when he steps out of the taxi, for a moment the headlights bloom behind him, and he hangs there in the dark, a whole day early, almost unrecognizable to me, a shadow of a man.

6

nside the house, I see the full extent of what happened to Rebecca in the mosh. There is a bruise with its own set of fingers around her neck, though in the half-light, it looks like residue from costume jewelry. We are all hungry. Eric empties his pockets, but his hands are shaking and a few soft Canadian bills fall to the floor. He stares into the fridge for a while, and then he piles some leftover steak onto a plate. Rebecca pits an avocado and motions for me to leave. On my way up the stairs, I hear Eric say, *What did you do to your hair*, his refusal to acknowledge me one of the many reminders that I am, in the grand scheme of things, an extremely brief addendum to their mortgage, to their marital bathrobes, to the two cars parked side by side. I sit at the top of the stairs and eavesdrop. When they begin to talk, it is in a very languid, businesslike fashion, their conversation filled with affirmations like *yes, I understand you*, and *yes, that is valid*, like they are a couple of aliens who have seen all the invasion agitprop and want to reiterate that they come in peace. This is actually much more unsettling than the alternative. Their hushed tones are polite and inorganic, Eric's effort so much more apparent than his wife's, and then in the middle of a digression about his experience with customs, he says, *what is she doing here, what are you doing*, and that tells me all I need to know, so I go to the guest room and start gathering my things. I look up the hours for my storage unit and scan the fine print for policies on habitation, but none of the language is clear. When I come out with my bag, Akila opens her door and motions for me to come inside. She takes my bag and tells me to take off my shoes.

"Your feet are horrible," she says, not looking at me, turning on the TV. I sit down on the floor and try to keep my flat, chronically dry feet out of view. "It's going to be all night."

"What?"

"Their dialogue," she says, a little annoyed, like she wishes I would keep up. "It's this thing they learned in therapy— Radical Candor." She makes a cross with her fingers. "It's an axis. There's also Ruinous Empathy, Manipulative Insincerity, and Obnoxious Aggression."

"I didn't know they were in therapy."

"Yeah. Sometimes we all go together. It's terrible." She mutes the TV and turns to me with a solemn look on her face. "It isn't perfect here, but it's fine. Please don't mess this up."

"Listen, I'm not here to ruin your life. This all just happened," I say, and she picks up her phone, opens Twitter, and gives a short, joyless laugh. She scrolls for a bit before turning her attention back to me.

"Because if I'm going to have to move again, I just want to

know. I have an insecure attachment style, and I *just* started calling them Mom and Dad. School is terrible, but I have my own room, and they let me close the door. I know you probably don't care, but—"

"I'm not a monster," I say, and she shrugs.

"I don't know that," she says. "I can't be sure of that. But I'm sure about this—it literally takes nothing for this all to go away. My last family was really happy. I had this fish tank, and it was inside the wall. So it felt permanent, even though it was probationary. And then Carol went to this residency in the woods and when she came back she didn't want to be married anymore. I didn't see it coming, and I usually do."

"I'm sorry," I say, and she pauses the stream, turns to look at me.

"That's such a weird thing to say. That you're sorry," she says. "I just don't want to have to do that again, okay?"

"Okay," I say, and she unpauses the show. It is a subtitled anime, the animation limber and bright, all the characters living in a vaguely Eastern European village that is under siege by nude giants. Everyone is screaming. A giant bounds into the village and puts his foot through a levee. A cavalry made entirely of teenagers takes the offensive, and then a second giant appears and drops a horse down his throat, the whinnying paired with a dramatic upskirt of a female colonel who is suddenly airborne with her double-hilted claymore, the arteries in the giant's neck spraying the upturned faces of the blacksmith and candlestick maker as I close my eyes.

Seven hours later, I wake up in a ball on Akila's floor. Akila is asleep in bed, a video game controller still in her hand. The room is dark but for the blue light of the television, where a save screen is on a loop. I turn off the TV and put the controller on top of the console. I take my bag and my shoes and go downstairs, the light at 5:00 a.m. soft and gray, the key hooks and baby tomatoes and silent digital clocks redefined by the single muddy bootprint on the floor. Rebecca's actual boots are not much farther off, their relationship to each other preserving the manner in which they were removed, which is without the use of the hands, one foot anchoring the other while it lifts out of the shoe. I take the tongue of the boot between my fingers, and when I pull them away they are coated in dust. I drink a few glasses of water and wander to the downstairs bathroom on the assumption that it will be empty, though when I open the door Eric is there shaving and listening to the weather report.

We look at each other through the mirror, and there are things I want to say, apologies and accusations that all convene into a strangled, inarticulate sound, though when he looks away and flicks the razor into the sink, when he turns up the weather report and continues as if I am not there, it surprises me, and immediately after the surprise comes disappointment for being caught off guard by a completely unsurprising thing, and when I catch my reflection in the mirror, I see how I am breathing through my mouth. I return to the guest bathroom, where I take a scalding shower and try to forget how I looked, the grime from the mosh making the water brown, more grass than seems possible coming out of my hair, the debris around the drain not enough to deter me from lying down in the tub and being dramatic, humiliation being such that it sometimes requires a private performance, which I give myself, and emerge from the shower in the next stage of hurt feelings. For me, this is denial.

I unpack my bag and arrange my belongings around the guest room. I sit at the kitchen table and drink coffee from my Captain Planet mug. Rebecca appears with wet hair. The tips of her ears are still tinted with dye. She fills a Tupperware container with fruit, puts it into a paper bag, and writes 305 *Calories* on the front. Akila runs down the stairs, takes the bag, and rushes out of the door. Outside I see the old woman who has been watching me. She opens her newspaper and looks up as one of the sheets takes to the air. Eric comes down the stairs with a suitcase and a piece of tissue above his lip. He doesn't acknowledge me, and I go to my room and apply the fentanyl patch. I take a book from the small library in the living room. Thirty pages in, a duke, the black sheep of a dysfunctional Welsh duchy, is training a nearsighted handmaid in the tenets of aristocracy, crushing her bifocals beneath his boot and drawing her newly beautiful face into his hands. I try to busy myself. I do pushups, alphabetize the books. I raid the fridge and cobble a few sandwiches from what I can find. I wrap one of the sandwiches in wax paper. I get on a Manhattan-bound train. I arrive at the library full of regret. The fentanyl has upset my stomach, and I need to go to the bathroom. I make it all the way to a limited exhibit on Nile River Valley Linguistics and Gene Flow in Nubia before I realize I'm in the wrong place. I take a moment and look at the collection because I like the smell of the place. There is a large infographic on mtDNA types and population sampling. There is a Nubian drawing of a man, and though the drawing has no perspective, the color of the water around him is carefully preserved, and I think about the resilience of that single pigment, the lapis lazuli, traversing time.

I take a bus to the correct library, and inside, I can smell the natural decay, the fermentation, the glue and twine and leather, paper as it degrades and betrays its origin, reminds you it comes from the trees. The library is mostly empty, though the few people who are around are intent on their work, a group of college students looking through reference section O–P, a woman hunched over a microfiche machine. I circle each floor until I get to an exhibit on Wartime Cognitive Dissonance and the Physiology of Dissent. After a brief dedication to the donors, there is a succession of helmets, cracked, blown out, covered in names of wives, children, and wry condemnations of God, a Vietcong bicycle on display backlit by warm, orange light, photographs of soldiers cleaning their glasses and tuning transistors, the helicopter blades and jungle brush foiling the camera's aperture with movement and incomplete light, naked children and self-immolation and prisoners of war wilting on tarmacs, a daisy in the barrel of a gun having nothing on the unnatural look of a soldier's smile, the look of the incomplete synthesis of fight or flight and the limbic system when it cannot compute. My father only ever smiled like this, like every morning he had to put on his skin and adhere to a code of behavior he could no longer understand, a highly functioning collection of pathologies with shrapnel in his back.

He was years removed from his service by the time I was old enough to misplace his Purple Heart, but during prayer meetings and birthday parties, it was apparent he was different, molecularly, like some fundamental human component had either been emptied out or on bad days, cranked up to eleven, the Fourth of July or a person entering his room too silently grounds for a survival response so disproportionate that as a kid you struggle to understand the blind anger and periods of profound withdrawal, though when you go to see the fireworks with your mother and he isn't there, you understand that whatever keeps him away is scary, that it is sad. When my father was a soldier, his prefrontal cortex wasn't yet complete. He could not grow a full mustache, and when he came back home he had a cane and a DIY tattoo of a woman's name. The cane was mostly for show. The woman was his first wife, and my mother was his third.

He'd spent his formative years in various homes in the Bible Belt with grim aunts who could trace their American lineage to the original bill of sale. He kept chickens while his mother, the sibling his aunts didn't talk about, was in Louisiana slowly going mad. These were terms of art my father gave to me as I was learning to swim, his old man's vocabulary having none of the clinical tact of the DSM-5. There were asylums, there was madness, and in the place of Germans, there were Krauts. His mother did not have a chemical imbalance, she had something fickle, something female, and so she returned to him with a severed frontal lobe. He was afraid of her like I would one day be afraid of him, because children, like dogs, are attuned to the signs of an impending storm. He became a man who always had girlfriends but didn't much like them, a strapping sailor with a dampened drawl and a center part, his unruly hair slicked back with pomade. Then the war, shit and mud and some fusion of the two, the shipwreck's centrifuge and the axon unraveled to the center of the nerve, my father the civilian, alarming the neighborhood with his midnight walks, shining his medals and trying to fool doctors with a carefully crafted limp. While he collected disability, it was not enough, and he had done it, the thing that most animals do but which only a few animals grieve, he had been up close and found it fetid and strange, killing for his country—a country that, once he was back home, reminded him that patriots could be shell-shocked, could be spangled in Arlington grass, but absolutely could not be black. And after having walked around with a child's blood underneath his fingernails, at home the banks, the churches, the women, were nothing. He saw that the people at home did not see black men like him among them, that they were unprepared. So he came to New York armed only with confidence, and after two dead wives, my mother appeared before him on Broadway and 143rd, pretty and young and high.

At the end of the exhibit, I realize Special Collections is in the basement. I take the elevator down and my hands are shaking. I

take off the fentanyl patch and put it in my purse. In the basement, I look through a thick pane of glass and count a dozen
archivists. All of them are women. They don't wear uniforms
but they move uniformly, the microfilm and glass plate negatives poised in the hand without contact of the palm, the flatbed
scanners and DSLRs splashing their faces with light. Beyond
them, Eric removes his mask, pulls on a cotton glove. He opens
a book underneath a mounted light, and when he lifts the page
it is almost translucent, like onion skin. He beckons over the
archivist closest to him, motions to the binding. She removes
her mask and smiles. He puts his hand on her shoulder and how
great is that, that in this shabby library basement, he is warm
and involved, apparently the kind of boss who is also your
friend.

When I turn around there is a woman sitting at what a moment
ago was a vacant desk. She is a natural black girl, bright and
woowoo, a cluster of cloudy amethyst around her neck. She asks
me if I need help. I tell her that I need to speak with Eric, but
when I turn and look through the glass, he is gone. I tell her I
brought him a sandwich, and she looks me up and down and
tells me he is out.

I take the sandwich and stop at a Duane Reade. I buy a Snapple
and small bottle of Dr. Schulze's Intestinal Formula #2, which
boasts thirty-five million active cultures, and I ask for cash back.
I check my email and there is a message from Panera Bread that

reads, *While there are currently no open positions as this time, we encourage you to apply in the future*, a message from the Department of Education, from Bank of America, from my landlord, who has bad news about the security deposit, from a Nigerian prince, and from Blue Cross Blue Shield, which would like to remind me that per my firing, I will be uninsured in eleven days. On the bus back, I watch the road. The rain is heavy and there is a man running along the shoulder with a gas can in his hand. I think of my mother, who was sympathetic to a lot of things, to brown spider plants, to cats with alopecia, and most especially to car trouble. There was no hitchhiker she did not indulge, no man with a smoking Saab she was unwilling to help. Whenever I was in the car, I pleaded with her to keep going. I felt anxious around these men, and I struggled with what to say. But during her time as a dealer, an addict, and then a fervent Seventh-day Adventist, she was mellowed by the cosmic and by her prolonged chemical abuse, brimming with the grade of charisma you see in septuagenarian rock stars whose tepid late-career albums remind everyone they're still alive, charisma that exists at the end of a liver, that has to do with acceptance, which incidentally is a tenet of Narcotics Anonymous and the SDA faith, wherein death is inevitable and complete. Except as a pious child, I could not feel casual about death. I had read Ecclesiastes, and the idea of death as nothingness terrified me. We picked up a man and he had a Bible in his hands. My mom was thrilled by the synchrony, but a mile away from the exit, I looked in the back seat and he was touching himself.

I return to the house by noon and sit in the garden. I dig a hole and find a smooth gray stone. I wash it in the bathroom and hold it inside my mouth. In the end, I put it on the windowsill. I go to my room and masturbate angrily to that picture of Eric in Greece, and when it doesn't make me feel any better I wander around the house. Rebecca is asleep with the door open, and for a while I stand there and watch her. I take pictures of different items around the house—the KitchenAid, a bowl of nuts that are primarily nigger toes, a drawer of old duck sauce packets and pens. I take a few of the ballpoints and a couple of pieces of paper from the printer that has, for the length of my stay, remained unplugged. I retreat to my room and try to render the photos as realistically as I can. At three, I hear Akila come home from school and run up to her room. By the time Eric comes home, I have the KitchenAid down, though the beater looks a little weird. The house is quiet. When Eric was away, the house was filled with sound, Akila's and Rebecca's routines textured and discordant, water and glass, sticky sounds of trash and sparring gear and doorjambs swollen with heat, the mailman and the democratic socialist at the door, all the toilets at the mercy of a houseful of women, the sensory meridian of tangled jewelry, of bobby pins and linoleum, of dubbed anime and the neighbor's dog, otherwise a soft cosine of electricity and digital noise. With Eric home, there is none of that. I listen for any movement in the house, but none of it is distinct. There are no running faucets or noisy floorboards that precede feet. We all just materialize.

Halfway through a long shower, through the curtain, I see Eric's silhouette. I don't hear him come in, but I hear him lock the door. He stands there silently as I wash my hair. When I get out of the shower, he is gone.

The mornings are still and all the nights feel like Friday night, by which I mean they feel like the Sabbath, which, despite my hedonism, remains my body's central quartz. When I kept the Sabbath, I did not yet have breasts. There were VHS tapes of devout animated cucumbers and my mother's drawings of Lucifer, which bothered me until I had the vocabulary to know I was aroused. I was excited to explain the tenets of SDA to the kids in my new public school. I conceded that one of our early leaders invented cornflakes to treat masturbation, but asserted meditation on the natural environment as a form of self-love. It took a year before I realized my classmates' questions were a sport. I didn't take it personally. I tried harder, came to school with arguments already formed. A boy from the companion high school, an atheist who was four years my senior, pointed out my contradictions, and I went home and prepared more notes. The Sabbath itself was pristine. Of course I indulged loopholes. Sometimes I slept it away so I could avoid the boredom, sometimes I spent the day curating twelve-hour mixtapes of Christian rock. But most of the time, though I wasn't allowed to dance and knew that everyone was having fun without me, I liked the quiet, the languor of a single hour, of a day when you are deliberate, thankful for what was made deliberately, retina and turnips and densely coiled stars, things so complex I could barely render them in paint. Though some things are not complex. Some things are accidents, and this is how it was filed with the insurance company when my mother wrecked the car. She didn't come out of her room for four days. When I went inside, it smelled bad and she said that God was dead. My father took me to Friendly's. A waitress dropped a tray of sundaes while he was holding my hand, and he crushed my fingers at the noise. He referred to my mother's periods of catatonia as *moods*. He did not dare suggest we lift her up in prayer. Though he regaled each moony deaconess with stories of the work he'd done abroad, he did not pretend with me. My father did not believe in anything, and I was the only one who knew. To everyone else, my father was a God-fearing man. A charismatic servant with a troubled wife and a way of making women feel heard. On Friday nights such women would file into our home, and his office door would shut.

I talked to the atheist on the phone, at first about homework but then about other things. When I went to his house, he played King Crimson and I told him my mother did not believe in God. I kissed him on the mouth and he didn't kiss me back. I understood that I had engaged seriously with someone who only engaged theoretically, and I was so humiliated by this that we never spoke again.

Now I am different. I have learned not to be surprised by a man's sudden withdrawal. It is a tradition that men like Mark and Eric and my father have helped uphold. So I endure Eric's silence, even as our paths cross in the morning and in the middle of the night. I don't attempt to break it, though the longer it persists, the more it mutates. For a day or so, it becomes hilarious, and then a little erotic, a seething, suffocating thing that makes me aware of how long it's been since I've been touched. I could find a local man to tide me over, but it feels like too much work. I've already done the work with Eric. He knows when I got my first period and I know he is decent to waitstaff, and I'm not interested in sucking the cock of a stranger who has potentially made a waitress cry. There is only so much I can do to save face. I am living in their house and eating their food. I am running out of money and I don't know how long they will let this go on.

I try to be scarce. I spend my days making small still lifes of items in their house and playing video games with Akila, who favors console-based fighting where women disembowel each other with their bare hands. During these sessions, she is instructional but pitiless, adamant that I earn my win. We customize our costumes and weaponry and then she rips out my spine. In a week, I have calluses on my thumbs. I take the booklet and read through the character bios, each story originating with a single unlockable character who appears in the booklet as a silhouette. While we are in pursuit of this silhouette, Akila tells me that she does not like September, and in Louisiana, it is a big month for hurricanes. She says her mother was swept away in a flood. There is a FEMA jacket hanging in her closet and she used to wear it all the time, but after going to therapy for a while, she wears it only once a year.

I walk around the cul-de-sac, take long calls with Sallie Mae. I defer my student loans, schedule an appointment with a gastro-enterologist in Hackensack. In the waiting room, I scan through the requirements for public assistance, and when I see the doctor he puts his finger in my asshole and tells me that he thinks we should run more tests. When I tell him my insurance expires in four days, he prescribes an OTC osmotic laxative that I can stir into tea. He asks that I come back once I have insurance again, and the plea is so sincere that when I visit the pharmacy to pick up my prescription, I wander the vitamin aisle and cry.

I am relieved to find that there are no family dinners. It reminds me of home, how everyone eats in a different room. Akila downstairs in front of the TV. Rebecca in the kitchen, standing up. A few times I see Eric make his plate and disappear into the basement, which is the only place in the house that is locked. Rebecca joins me for coffee in the morning but doesn't talk. Most of the time she is either sleeping or in the morgue. With Eric in the house she is dimmer, more exact, her circuit brief and preordained, this clockwork so particular it feels precarious, vulnerable to a single, badly chosen word. I want to talk about how things were before Eric came back. How it has been two weeks since I rinsed the dye from her hair, and there are still traces of it between the bathroom tiles.

When the house is empty I take more photos of her things. With the last thirty dollars in my account I buy a twelve-count tin of Prismacolors and thick vellum bristol board. At night I open my window and work from the pictures, from the procession of glass and alloy and silk, textures defined principally by their fickle relationship to light and so as difficult to render as digital joints, her perfume a cold, narrow palette, her jewelry warm and wide, her clothes a little bit of both, the expression of weft and grain not dissimilar to hair. In between these sketches, there is a house. Clapboard and brass and turf, and even in this I see them, but I cannot see myself. For the first time I can capture knuckles and plastic, but there is the issue of my face. I still can't manage a self-portrait. When I try, there is a miscommunication, some synaptic failure between my brain and my hand. I try to find another way toward the self-portrait. I close my door and destroy my room and take a picture of the mess. I approach the drawing optimistically, but I am not there. The next time the house is clear, I take an opposite tack and clean. I take out the garbage and then I take a picture of the bags on the curb. I clean the bathroom and take a picture of the tongue of hair I pull from the drain, and at night I render these pictures, hoping to see myself. When I don't, when I have completed a series on folded laundry and grout and still am not there, I keep cleaning. And then one morning while I am shining the faucets, Rebecca tells me she is planning a party and she would like me to help. It is a

party for Akila that Akila does not want. Akila says this explicitly as we are making our way through a new game, a turn-based
RPG where the protagonist is an army mail clerk with amnesia.
His only memory is of a boy from a small mountain town. As we
draw closer to the first conflict of the war, the base is flanked by
a long, alpine shadow. The non-playable characters are not
subtle about it. A colonel whose pockets we emptied earlier in
the game points to the shadow and says, *Was that there before?*
As we climb the mountain, Akila says that Rebecca is throwing
her a birthday party. She says that she would rather spend it
alone. The controller vibrates in her hand. The vibration indicates the genesis of a new memory, a woman who is trying to
put out a fire.

But Rebecca cannot be dissuaded. On Sunday we pile in the
truck and drive to the skating rink. We park at the back entrance
and bring the decorations inside. The rink appears to be owned
by a happy family. Not one of them is over five feet tall. The father tries to be friendly as Eric is calibrating the helium tank, but
this task has become so complicated that Eric's laughter, which
is meant to be polite, comes out more as an honest indication
that he would like the man to go away. Though this was her
idea, Rebecca is not much better. She bites her nails as one of
the family's teenage children explains the regulations of the
party room. While I set out the napkins and paper plates, she is
on the phone. She is talking in a low, threatening voice with the
mothers of Akila's guests, who all seem to have called with last-
minute news. All the while, Akila is there, helping with the

crepe and streamers. Her wig shifts when she bends down to put on her skates. Eric goes over to her and helps her tie them, and though my relationship with my father was not ideal, I recognize the look that passes between them, a look that is conspiratorial, that temporarily eschews the boundary between parent and child for the recognition of some mutual misery, in this case, a birthday party that neither of them wants to attend. The by-product of this alliance is that it often throws the other parent under the bus as a matter of course, though as a kid, this is what makes it great. When I was young, I didn't understand it was cruel. My father's remarks about my mother's moods and Bible studies felt innocuous and brought some air in the room, his ambivalence about God appearing to be a welcome bit of levity as opposed to what it really was—a profound vacuum in the place where God used to go. During the years he killed for his country, he'd killed God, too, and he came back home inspired to make one of his own.

Only two kids show up. They arrive at the same time and look at each other as it dawns on them that they are the only ones. And they are late. Rebecca runs out of the party room with bloody fingernails and confetti in her hair and ushers them into the room where Akila is waiting in a blue party hat. There is another party across the hall composed entirely of senior citizens, and they are extremely loud. When Rebecca goes over to ask if they can keep it down, they say that no, they cannot. Members from the happy family keep popping in to ask if we are expecting more guests, and after a query from the smallest son, Eric emerges from his dark corner and says *This is it, okay*, and he doesn't yell, but he is large and the optics are not great. The two guests make a valiant effort to talk to Akila, but the conversation always seems to fizzle out. The guests begin talking only to each other. And no one can tell what the piñata is supposed to be. Akila spends three minutes making direct contact, and though I have watched her break through boards with ease, the piñata won't give. Eventually Rebecca just rips it down from the ceiling and tears it open with her hands. As she is doing this, the mother from the happy family comes in with the cake and the number of candles is wrong. At this point, everyone in the room has become so attuned to Rebecca's growing fury that, upon the revelation about the candles, the room holds its collective breath. Rebecca stands motionless before the cake. For a while nothing happens, and then Eric laughs. And then Akila laughs and the room follows suit. High on having dodged that particular bullet, we all put on our skates and head out into the rink. The neighboring party is already out and having a time. It is three in the afternoon and they are all drunk. Akila goes out and skates by herself, and I roll up beside her so she won't be alone, but she feels my charity and skates away. The neighboring party keeps giving the DJ candy bars, and so between the Spice Girls and Drake there is Paul Anka and Nat King Cole. Rebecca is making a show of having fun. She skates circles around Eric and tries to get him to play along, but he is very unstable and sticks to the sides. And of course, there is disco. The big ones—"YMCA" and "Bad Girls" and "Ain't No Stoppin' Us Now," songs that have transcended genre into concept, songs you don't so much listen to as project your memory onto the wax, songs so fascistically joyful that when "That's the Way" comes on I have no choice but to look at Eric to see if he is remembering with me, and he is not. He is on the side of the rink, looking at something on his phone. As "Whip It" emerges out of "Smoke Gets in Your Eyes," a chipped disco ball descends from the ceiling. But something is wrong. The motorized arm strains, and when I look over to the happy family, they are all craned over the dashboard by the register, readjusting the dials. Everyone pauses to watch, and so when the chain snaps, it does not feel like a technical failure so much as a deference to our collective will. Akila is waiting with outstretched arms. The force of it buckles her knees. She cradles the ball against her chest and looks into the glass. A stunned murmur ripples through the crowd, and everyone is still as she moves, her face dappled in the ball's recycled light. It makes me think of the first time I saw her, the way she seemed slightly unreal, like a glitch, with her dark eyes and shiny, synthetic hair. Now, the dissonance feels dire. It weighs me down as I watch her glide to the edge of the rink, set the ball down, take off her skates, and ask if she can go home.

At home, we disperse to our separate rooms. Akila's gifts, which were hauled out of the party room and back into the truck, sit unopened in the dining room. At midnight, Akila knocks on my door. She says she has reason to believe that the woman who is trying to put out the fire is the mail clerk's mother. Since the mail clerk doesn't engage in direct combat, his HP depends entirely on the successful management of his mood. To keep it stable, we visit the mess tent and talk the NPCs to the end of their script, though bad selections can be more damaging than doing nothing at all. If we have coffee instead of tea. If we engage the lieutenant and he shows us a photo of his dog. I suggest that we try opening the mail, but his mood is not high enough to absorb the illegality and it kills him instantly. I get up to leave, but Akila calls my name. She considers me and then removes her wig. She puts it down on the floor inside out, and there is a tag sewn between the weft that says *Party Supply*. Then I look at her, and for a moment, I assume she is wearing a wig cap, but it is her scalp, exposed and covered in chemical scars.

"You let it stay in too long," I say.

"I thought it was supposed to burn," she answers, and this too is part of that common tongue. Sodium hydroxide and the real estate of the scalp. The first time I lost my hair, I was ten and no one was home. My hands were too small for the gloves that came in the box, and the relaxer, bought in secret at a sparse, upstate Beauty Supply, singed the back of my neck. I hid the hair I'd lost in a bin near the community pool, and once my mother realized what had generated my new interest in scarves, she didn't talk to me for a week. I go to my room and find my shea butter, jojoba oil, and silk scarf. When I return, I have her sit between my knees so that I can have a closer look, and I notice that in the hair she still has, her curls are still intact. She says that she panicked. That she wanted to be different for the party. As I wrap the scarf, I am too aware of her head. I am aware of her skull, of the vulnerability of her thirteen-year-old bones. I leave the oil and shea on her dresser, and for a while I am unable to sleep. Because she is thirteen, and I remember how it felt from the inside. I remember what I thought I knew about people, and the pride I took in being alone. But from the outside, the loneliness is palpable, and I think, *She is too young.*

The silence persists. Eric pays me another visit while I'm in the shower, and this time I don't hear him until the lights are off. I can't tell how close he is to the curtain, or if he is even still there, but I act as if he is. I touch myself and wonder if he is listening. For a few weeks I continue my series of "self-portraits." I only take things they are unlikely to miss. A lightbulb, a dinner plate, a single winter glove. Things I can crush or hang over a flame, though these portraits of shards and ash ultimately feel less truthful than when I render areas of the house I have thoroughly cleaned. I try to be inconspicuous, but on the night I get into the HVAC unit with a toothbrush, Rebecca comes down the stairs in scrubs and tells me there is a unit on the other side of the house. I can't tell if she is serious, or if this acknowledgment is meant to make me stop. And as a matter of principle, I stop for a few days. When we cross paths I try to discern from her face whether this is the intended result. But eventually I find myself on the other side of the house, brushing dust out of the vents.

The next morning, there is money on my dresser. I close the door and count it. I pocket it and buy more art supplies—raw canvas, stretcher bars, Lascaux gesso—and some tea tree oil for

Akila. I take the bus to the library, and I sit in the stacks and count the change. Like bone, the money—the paper and nickel and zinc—feels more mutable when held inside the hand. It feels finite, tethered to the source in a way that makes it explicitly transactional, and so of course it is demeaning. But it is also demeaning to be broke. I go down to Special Collections and watch the archivists through the glass. They are capturing a three-dimensional image of a gilded urn. Between the softboxes and umbrellas, they place the urn on a polyester wheel. One archivist turns the wheel, and another captures the image. However, the archivist at the wheel is older and has a tremor in her hand. As they are reaching the last sixty degrees, she loses her place. Eric comes out from his office, smiles, and picks up where she left off. He looks through the glass and holds my eye for a long moment, and then he turns and disappears into his office. Upstairs, I look through the death certificates. I find a certificate for a man who fell out of a window while trying to prove to a tour group that it was made of unbreakable glass, for a man who fell into a machine in a textile mill and suffocated in eight hundred yards of wool, for a man who was crushed by a trash compactor while looking through a dumpster for his phone, and the usual, the strokes, the cancers, the suicides. I look for my father's certificate, and though I don't find it, I find four Ivan Darbonnes who died in New York between 1975 and 2018. All of them died in Brooklyn. My father died in Syracuse, five years after my mother. We hadn't talked in six months, partly because we were (comfortably) estranged, and partly because his new wife was screening my calls. The last time I saw him, two years before his death, he took the Metro-North into the city and we saw a matinee of the newest Aronofsky. After, we went for dinner and he kept saying things were expensive, but occasionally he would pause and tell me what he thought the movie meant. He'd stopped eating sugar and carried around a gallon of his own "chemically altered" water, and before we saw the movie I had to stuff it in my purse. He'd grown skinny and gullible. I lost my patience with him while we were waiting for the downtown A. I yelled at him about electrolytes and we were silent on the train. And then a few years later, I was checking Facebook and I noticed all the condolences on his page.

I stop cleaning altogether for a couple of weeks, but the money still comes. It comes in a sealed white envelope and the amount is different every time. One hundred dollars. Forty-eight dollars and fifteen cents. Three hundred dollars during a week I don't do anything at all. I deposit the money quietly, spend some of it on an expensive bottle of polyethylene glycol. I take Akila to get her first protective style. We take the train into the city and find an African braiding parlor on 125th. It smells right, like yaki and hibiscus and lavender oil. Above the Malaysian bundles, a Trinidadian soap opera is on. When the actors speak, you can hear the air in the room. Three women work on Akila at once. They hook in the yaki and speak softly to each other in Queen's English. Every thirty minutes a man comes in and asks for cash. When he is gone, one of the hairdressers asks me to pay before he comes back. She says he is her boyfriend. Four hours later, a woman comes out with a pot of boiling water to seal the ends of the Senegalese twists. They soak Akila's shirt on the train back, and at home she changes into something dry.

"A new do! Very nice!" Eric says to Akila when he passes by her room. He lingers in the doorway and asks how much time it took and makes a joke about how heavy her head must feel. He mentions a black woman at work who always changes her hair, and he asks a slew of slightly invasive questions with this bright, apologetic look on his face. I have had this exact exchange more times than I can count, but I can't tell if Eric is trying so hard because he is white, or if it is because he is a dad. When he leaves, Akila looks at me and laughs.

I look through my self-portraits, and I can't see myself, but I am well acquainted with every corner of the house. A habit has been built. I clean all the windows in the house, polish the silver, smoke a few cigarettes. I lie around in the dark and indulge all the bright half-dreams, the speed and pavement, the staggered lips of cliffs and yawning desert. I wander around the house after midnight and find the door to Rebecca and Eric's bedroom slightly ajar, and they are having what is, in their case, aptly called sexual intercourse. It does not look like porn but still defies description, Eric enormous and rectangular, Rebecca feral and smooth. Regrettably, they are beautiful, and per their soft chatter and tender readjustment, at least a little bit in love. I take a few photos with my phone, and I check the time. I want to go to bed, but I feel obligated to stay until they finish, and when they do, Rebecca rolls over and turns up the TV.

I return to my room, scroll through the pictures, and do

three preliminary sketches. I touch myself and try to imagine what it is like to have comfortable, familiar sex, to be pounded sweetly as James Corden does his monologue. I wake up in the afternoon, walk two miles to the rink and get some soft-serve ice cream, feed a pretzel to a pigeon with an atrophied leg. I go to the mall and play the arcade games they keep in the food court, and, after talking to a Sears associate about all-terrain tires, I buy a blue dress.

At home, I put on the dress and for the first time in a while, I feel like a person someone might want to kiss. I sit in front of the mirror and apply makeup, my hand unsteady and the kohl too heavy around my eyes. I put on lipstick, scrub it off, and then put it on again. I watch Rebecca drive away and I go down to the basement, where Eric is looking through the largest collection of vinyl I have ever seen. When I see him, I feel short of breath, and I pause on the stairs and consider turning back. He glances at me and pulls a record from a thick, plastic sleeve. All of it is coordinated and strategically filed, shrink-wrapped and, in some cases, refrigerated, all the dials set to fifty-five, all of twelve-inch Philadelphia funneling into the derivative and French, into the 4/4 and South Bronx, the minimalist German records most apparently handled, the entire room kind of hairy and out of time with the dirty shag and wood paneling and green La-Z-Boy. He lets the needle down, and I continue my silent tour as something is made of the polymer and spiral groove, something preserved but ultimately Jurassic, the sound opaque and full of grain, which I understand as a function of authenticity and also as a condemnation of my ears, which find this cool but mostly just okay. He hands me a glass of gin and wipes the lipstick off my face with the back of his hand. The gin is warm, and the record is Brazilian and very reliant on the theremin. He pours himself a drink and circles the room, pausing only to fuss with the player, which is a beautiful machine but within this context a stark digression with its digital numbers and sleek, aluminum deck. No record is right. At the two-minute mark, Eric swaps one out for another, and then again, the interval between records smaller each time, so that by the fifth it is an erasure, the business of replacing the vinyl bracketing the lyric and unresolved brass. When he finds a record that is satisfactory, he crosses the room and pushes me into the wall. He rolls up his sleeve and wraps his hand around my throat, a thoughtful, preliminary squeeze, as if the hand is not his own. He tries the other hand, and this one, the left one, seems to be the one he prefers. He says, *You want this*, like it is a question and then like it is a statement, and the most immediate cost of our two-week silence is that I have forgotten his voice, which now seems too soft and too high. Up close, every detail is slightly diminished. The assessment is mutual. His hand slackens as he searches my face for where the memory became corrupt, and then his hand tightens, becomes deliberate, each one of his fingers jointed and distinct, everything reduced and anatomical, my cartilage and salivary glands explicit, my breath half-drawn and made into something sharp and unexpressed in my chest. That I can't breathe does not immediately feel like a problem. There are things happening in the interim, a door opening upstairs, an eyelash on his cheek, and before he fully commits to the grip, he lifts the glass of gin from my hand. *Thank you*, I almost say. But my voice is gone, and the room is gone, though on my way out I notice that the record has begun to skip.

7

n the weeks that follow, we are new. There is some attempt at an apology he doesn't mean and that I don't want, and then we stand at different windows and wait for Rebecca to drive away. He lets himself into my room and we trip over ourselves while we undress, the contact tenuous and inexact, kisses spoiled by fervor, full of air and teeth and always off the intended mark, though I am just happy to be touched. We wait for the moments Akila and Rebecca are not home, but ardor is a kind of negligence. Rooms are chosen indiscriminately and sometimes doors are not properly closed. The days are shorter in October, and we take full advantage of the nights.

We don't talk about what brought us here, the spontaneous asphyxiation hanging between us like a silent, low-gravity dream. Instead we meet in the dark, and all the wholly unoriginal, too generous things men are prone to saying before they come sound startling and true. Tender, silly words. Vocabulary you receive as a good sport and volley back with your eyes closed. Because when it is over, when he is bending over to collect his pants, there is a world beyond the door with traffic and measles and no room for these heady, optimistic words.

We have abbreviated dinners in Princeton and Hoboken. I draw an anchor on his forearm and the rest of the night we pretend that he will soon be at sea. We go to Paulus Hook in Jersey City and watch party boats cut slick circles around flat, brown barges, and when the water stills, he tells me that he will write me a letter every day. We always arrive home separately. When Rebecca is home, our conversations are curt and about insignificant things, about weather and whether the coffeepot should be cleaned, but as we develop this careful, mundane language, it becomes its own intimacy, the laundry and the miscellany beneath the silverware an irony that softens his face as he pulls my dress over my head. Of course, I am waiting for the other shoe to drop. Bobby pins are left behind, and a crystal centerpiece is destroyed. We crawl around in our underwear and try to find all the broken glass. Eric says he will come up with an explanation, but Rebecca does not seem appeased. She says there is a shard in her foot, and she talks about it for a week. She says she can't remove it, and sends me to the store for peroxide and gauze. When I look at her foot, nothing is there. *Look closer*, she says, and the next time Eric and I go out, I suggest we get a room.

I feel Rebecca reassessing my presence in their house. While I have learned how to use a mop and maintained the appearance of tutoring their daughter in the Pineapple Method and everything else African American 101, my résumé has been revised so frequently that my career in publishing and soft cheese has become a career in scientific journalism, the zebrafish trials at Sloan Kettering surprisingly easy to riff about over the phone, though not as easy in person when the interviewer, a distant relation of Jonas Salk, wants to talk about the moral implications of giving mice cocaine. During my interview with CVS, I try to be convincing in my assurance that pointing young adults in the direction of Plan B has always been a part of my five-year plan, but after the interview I go to the parking lot to drink some cough syrup and notice one of the managers watching me from his car.

And the money is still coming. It appears on my dresser with no indication of who it is from. I spend the money on paint and deposit the rest. I am tempted to ask Eric during the times we are together if it is him. If it is, I worry our relationship will become transactional, not in the way it already is, re: my twenty-something pussy and his fraying telomeres, but in the way I might have to parse the irregularity of the payments, the four hundred dollars one week, and the measly five the next, and confront the inconsistencies in my performance.

Eric takes off from work so we can have a picnic. I see him before he sees me. He is on his hands and knees smoothing the

wrinkles from the picnic blanket, and there is something so un-
dignified about this that I return to the bus stop and come back
in ten minutes when he is waiting with a bottle of wine. When
I sit down, he takes my face into his hands and I can feel the
salary in them, the forty-plus years of relative ease. He arranges
the crudo and the cheese and I roll a loose, dry joint. When we
light it, the cherry tears through the paper and we pass it back
and forth like an emergency. Just as it begins to rain, a 747 slants
toward Newark. He pulls me into his lap, and it is all a little
weirder in the afternoon when he can see my face. I fall back
onto the blanket and feel the sun on my arms. I think to ask him
about the money, but he is kissing my palms, telling me about a
family picnic when he found out he was allergic to silver. We
drain the bottle, and he tells me that his parents are alive and still
together, that in his old suburb outside Milwaukee, there was a
genuine neighborhood witch, who in Norse tradition is called a
völva, and that she gave him his first guitar. I tell him about the
last birthday gift I received from my mother, a Polaroid camera,
and I slide the ring from his hand and put it into my mouth. For
a moment he watches, flushed and happy as I taste the alloy and
the sweat, but then he straightens and tells me that I always go
too far. We leave separately and at home we don't talk. I haven't
forgotten to ask him where the money is coming from, it's just
that I realize I hope it's coming from Rebecca.

She is mostly inaccessible. Up in the morning crushing Ambien
into her coffee and complaining about the neighbor's dog, out at
night when a new veteran comes into the morgue. There are

moments our contact feels thoughtful, the organic tampons that appear in my bathroom bound in twine, the want ads that appear on my vanity along with a red pen. There are also moments when I am reminded that her generosity comes with an asterisk. The way all her questions are instructions, texts asking if I can stay in my room while she meditates, queries about whether or not I know how to use a lawn mower and the cotton mask she gives me when I say the smell of fresh-cut grass makes me sick. *It's a death rattle*, she says, directing me to the lawn mower and adjusting the string on the mask, *the grass communicating its distress*, and for the rest of the day I think of that, sick to my stomach, the lawn buzzed and alkaline, the vinegar in the wine and carnage in the dew, everywhere the perfume of things that want to live.

I stay up until I have the living room TV to myself, and halfway through a *Rocko's Modern Life* marathon Rebecca comes home from work and falls asleep beside me, still in her boots and scrubs. At 1:00 a.m., when the Nicktoons segue into black and white, Rocky and Bullwinkle are in an air balloon and I move closer to her and she smells of formaldehyde and cigarettes, her hair damp and newly blond at the roots. I think of how my palms were dark for days after I dyed her hair. I lower the volume on the TV and watch her. She is like me, ordinary, prone to stretches where she looks bad, though unlike me, when she looks bad she looks soluble, her inertia fevered, Victorian. When the cartoon block loops back around and Jane Jetson shoots into space, I get up to leave and Rebecca grabs my wrist.

You should be grateful, she says, the light from the TV illuminating her face, *you have all the time in the world.*

When the house is quiet, sometimes I put some newspaper on the floor and mix paint. I put on the post office episode of *Mister Rogers' Neighborhood*, and I collect my staple gun and stretcher bars. Sometimes I turn my phone off and hope that when I turn it on there will be terrible news beyond the assassinations I breathlessly await, something hurtling through space, an untethered moon or sleek machine full of race-ending cephalopods. Otherwise, there are things to paint. Rebecca's boots and her half-eaten Granny Smiths, Rebecca in the garden, the six grainy pictures I took of Eric and Rebecca a month before.

On film it is even less abstract, even more anatomical, his scrotum and her knees, though there is a tenderness that gives me pause. I try to paint it, but none of the renditions are true. They are lurid and embarrassing in their attempt at scale. I have seen both Eric and Rebecca in various states of undress—Eric's hard torso and heterosexual underwear, Rebecca as most people see their mothers about the house, the harried bits of nudity between terry cloth and the single functional hook of a Playtex bra—but this is different, proof they are more than where they have ended up. I wish it would stop. Every Tuesday, 11:00 p.m., Conan O'Brien on TBS. On these nights I let myself into Akila's room and slip on a headset. I reload my rifle and clear German soldiers from the town church. I can't get out of

Normandy. My weapons are low-level and high-recoil and my avatar has tinnitus. After a blast, my controls stall and I have to wait until the ringing stops. Akila looks up from her computer and sighs, which is her passive-aggressive way of reminding me there are nobler gaming pursuits, games that require me to talk to villagers, that ask me to go out of my way to recruit crucial party members, but that have nothing on the instant gratification of blowing an enemy bunker to smithereens. *Nigger!* a kid from the Netherlands yells as a paratrooper falls from the sky. I slip off my headset, and Akila and I resume preparing for Comic Con, which, as she reminds me frequently, is two weeks away.

After we secure the tickets, Akila announces that she will be going to the con as an ifrit. There are immediate speed bumps— adapting the form of a canonically male Arabic fire lord to the body of a thirteen-year-old girl, fashioning armor and horns, and, in general, minding the mild body dysmorphia of a newly minted teenager. She pins a picture of an ifrit to the back of her door and measures her thighs. In its most common iteration, the costume is little more than a loincloth, and even with our adjustments, the costume is more skimpy than either Rebecca or Eric would like. However, because they have noticed Akila's burgeoning disdain for her body, they don't want to say anything to make it worse. Eric and Rebecca meet in the garden and have a hushed conversation about whether or not their reservations are unfeminist. I sit by my window and listen as Rebecca builds a case for opaque stockings and Eric frets about his whiteness and Akila's agency. *We can't let her do whatever she wants just because she's black*, Rebecca says. *That isn't intersectional feminism, it's bad parenting.* Despite Rebecca's protests, the cosplay moves along as planned, because ultimately both Eric and Rebecca are reluctant to tamper with the special climate that has made their somber daughter prone to smile. She comes to dinner and talks at length about how Stan Lee fought publishers over Spider-Man, how publishers did not feel it was feasible for a superhero to be a lower-middle-class kid from Queens, and she keeps a ledger of her calorie intake in a notebook with her Comic Con schedule, which is a persnickety thirteen-column document in cramped color-coordinated script.

Eric and I drive to Joann Fabrics and get four yards of brown pleather and a pound of multipurpose foam. We shop with our palms, sampling stiff brocade and hairy cashmere, and we look at each other to confirm if we are feeling the same thing. We try to make fire. He is not an artistic man, but he is a particular one, so serious about our materials that he stays up to make a call to a Chinese latex distributor that sent canary yellow instead of marigold. We stockpile mixed media in various yellows and reds, ask ourselves if we want the fire to be interactive or decorative. Eric asks Akila to join us on a trip to an archive in Mahwah, and when we get there, two archivists are waiting in a back room with an Arabic manuscript. They provide cotton gloves and between the steepled script there is an image of an ifrit razing a Persian town. Eric smiles as Akila goes carefully through the book, and back in the car he seems relieved. When we get home and Akila is out of the car, he turns to me and says that he needs this to be perfect. He says that Rebecca didn't want to adopt and he wonders if Akila can feel it. We brainstorm more iterations of fire—cardboard, string lights, a rope of knotted handkerchiefs—and we only see Rebecca in passing, as she is on her way out for work.

The next day, Rebecca can't find her ring. She and Eric talk for a while in the car, and when they come back inside, she is jubilant. Eric is less so. He assigns portions of the house to each of us, and we conduct a thorough search. As I'm looking underneath the couch, Akila comes down the stairs and glares at me. I go upstairs and Rebecca is reading a book in bed. Later in the week, Eric makes a down payment for a new one. He tells me the dollar figure, and it takes the air out of my lungs. He says he can't afford it, but what he means is that it is a pain. And Rebecca knows what she wants, a marquise diamond on a white gold band, bracketed by musgravite and citrine. On an evening when she has to work, she asks me to check on it, just to see how it's coming along. I go to the jeweler, and no one asks if I need help. I ask about the ring, and they say they are not authorized to show it to me. They watch me closely until I leave, and in the morning I tell Rebecca that it looked beautiful.

A few days later, Eric books a room at the Jersey City Marriott for the afternoon, and there are a few things happening downstairs that have put him in a bad mood, a conference on constitutional law and a K–8 concert that involves a popular squirrel character. The lobby is full of lawyers and kids on leashes. He takes a call from his assistant, who is managing a fiasco that has to do with a shipment of acetate film. *Are you saying we are dealing with vinegar syndrome*, he says as I undress. He hangs up the phone and sets his shoes by the door. He examines me with the back of his hand, and without the palm, the contact is remote, a quiet scrutiny I try to meet casually, though I am insecure about my breasts, which hang apart and feel deadened when I am not turned on. He asks me to take off his watch and I do it, clumsily, as he peers at my face. I try not to be worried by his expression, but he wears it even after he removes his pants, the searching look of a person who keeps finding nothing, which gives me the impression that the nothing is me. There is too much foreplay, a salvo of businesslike kisses that feel less like kisses and more like place setting, the fork and the spoon, and his fingers operating all the reliable dials. But he can't get hard. I do my best. An endless hand job and obliterated bicep, the condescending suction of a hopeful but ultimately futile blow job, and the desperate wish that sometime this all will end. When it does I lie next to him and think of the pictures, the soundless rutting of husband and wife. I squeeze his shoulder, and when he pushes my hand away I am relieved.

After an hour of trying to find something on TV, we go downstairs and sneak into the concert. The kids have been let off their leashes and are crowding the stage during a soft techno prelude to "London Bridge Is Falling Down." When the lights come up, a seven-foot-high papier-mâché Big Ben is there with two enormous, functional human hands. Behind it, there is a projection of a throbbing London Eye. When Eric passes me a flask, I notice Big Ben is telling the correct EDT. There are parents, zoned out or pathologically alert, a man using his wife's back to sign some papers, a woman pumping milk next to the hot dog cart.

The squirrel turns out to be animatronic, but when he comes out, the hall erupts, and a few kids need to be carried away. Eric and I are trying to be cool about it, but as we pass the gin back and forth it turns out that "Wheels on the Bus" is not so bad at 150 bpm, and while we are not the target demographic, we are stunned by the squirrel, whose eyes are dark and wet. When Eric looks at me, I know we are somehow having the same thought, which is that kids these days have never had to see the prototypes, and now the uncanny valley is gone.

Back in our room, we are both mellowed. He opens the window and puts the radio on, and we smoke a flat joint I find in the bottom of my purse. He keeps saying he doesn't feel anything, but then he takes a comb out of his briefcase and spends a while putting different parts in his hair. He comes back from the bathroom with a middle part and takes me into his arms, and all the faucets are on. There is a song on the radio that he likes, some supermarket standard that was big in the eighties, and I am coming to the realization that he is high and I am not. I've pulled too hard on an insufficient joint and I feel the exertion behind my eyes. He asks me to dance with him, but the song is bad. I think you need to have been alive in the eighties to like the music. I think you need a specific neural groove, a pane of nostalgia to sweeten what is sexless and extroverted and most suited for the mall. Still, I dance with him, though with the lights up I can't relax. I try to make it funny, but then I see Eric's disappointment and I don't know what to do with my hands. He asks me to stop and tells me to lie facedown. I ask him if something is wrong, and he hoists me up and takes me from behind as a sleepy radio voice is introducing "Come On Eileen." *You have nowhere else to go*, he says. He asks me to say it back to him.

"I have nowhere else to go," I say, and when it's over, he takes a shower for a long time, and then he apologizes profusely. He tells me that as a kid he had intricate immune deficiencies that sometimes forced him to keep his teddy bear in a jar, and it is this same immune response that dampens his ability to produce sperm. Because this deserves reciprocation, I tell him I got an abortion around the same time I learned to shoot a gun. I tell him more about the Polaroid camera I received from my mother, how for weeks I took photos of trees and telephone wire before I turned the lens on her. How she was a willing subject, until she saw what she looked like in the photos and asked me to stop. How I thought her resistance was petty and vain, a boring thing I'd seen less interesting adult women do, then I looked at the pictures and knew that she was right. She wasn't simply unphotogenic. She was bare in a way that film betrayed so dramatically that she became grotesque.

At home, we create a flank of fire with red and yellow tulle. Akila drapes it over her shoulders and shreds newspaper for the papier-mâché. Eric brings up some vinyl and we shape the horns to "Dancing Queen," though we are deep into ABBA's lesser-known songs by the time we fashion the breastplate from foam. After the hot glue dries, we go outside and spray-paint it silver. Akila shows me her archive of comic books, and aside from a few that I am not allowed to touch, I am free to browse. They vary in condition and age—thin newsprint issues with ads for milk and Tekken, *Girlfrenzy!* issues that skew more female, and incidentally a little more butch, older issues openly courting Generation X, between the ads for Gap and Gushers the grungy, long-haired Gothamite that is Bruce Wayne's son, a coked-up twentysomething cramped by his dad's Depression-era style.

Eric and I make more mistakes. Most notably the first (and last) time Eric calls me baby, which happens as he is trying to direct my attention to the mail, and which I can see he immediately wants to take back, because it feels preposterous, and because, we realize a moment later, Rebecca is in the room. The next day, we meet for lunch at a Wyndham in Teaneck and I arrive back at the house and find Rebecca crouched in the garden with her trowel. She picks through the fennel and lavender with her hands and inspects her palms. She says it was meant to be a butterfly garden, but this season a few things have gone wrong. The flowers came up pollen-poor and the population of natural predators was high. Curious deer. Beetles and spiders waiting in the daisies for painted ladies and red admirals. Hummingbirds deterred by sterile lilies. Now the garden is full of weeds and exoskeletons. Rebecca takes her trowel and starts prying out the weeds. I ask if she wants any help, and she says that she is fine. Her T-shirt is damp, yellow in the pits. She talks to herself, calls it opportunistic growth. She goes in with her shears and starts trimming around the lavender, but by the time she gets to the river mint, she is pulling it all up with her hands.

"I feel like I am the only one who hears that dog," she says, and it is only after she mentions it that I hear the baying. "We bred them like that. We made them needy and physically unfit. They used to be wolves. Now there are pugs with asthma."

"I never understood the appeal. Of pugs."

"I saw your paintings," she says, reaching for the peat moss. She has kindly kept her back turned, but still my lunch, the room service, is rising into my mouth.

"Which ones?"

"All of them," she says, and naturally I can only think of the most damning ones, paintings I went to great lengths to hide. Paintings that are reconnaissance, that are longing, and disproportionately of her. Somehow, I also wish I had been there, to see her when she saw herself in them.

"What did you think?" I ask, and she looks over her

shoulder, her face flushed and mean. I can't tell if she is looking at me or the neighbor's dog.

"I think they need work."

When everyone is asleep, I look through the paintings and hate myself. I do my best to avoid Rebecca, which is easy as she has all but disappeared. Veterans from the Silent Generation have been dying en masse, and when she is not at work she is asleep. I find myself listening for the sounds of her coming home. Then as I am working on another failed self-portrait I realize I am late. I check my menstruation app and scroll until I find the last little red teardrop, logged sixty-two days before, under which I have entered a short note—*the news is terrible today. Wish I was a man. Need more gesso and ultramarine.* So I go to my closet, collect a few wire hangers, and sort out the clothes I have been keeping on the floor. I clean my palette with my fingernails and arrange the dried acrylic into a color wheel that turns out to be dominated by incremental iterations of blue. I lie in bed and wonder how women don't feel it, the exact moment their bodies begin to create.

The next week, Rebecca insists I attend Akila's belt ceremony and makes no mention of the paintings. When I get in the car, Eric looks at me as if it were my idea. At the ceremony, he calls me Edith and sits as far away as he can. Akila does not receive her belt. Fifteen steps in, she forgets her form and excuses herself from the mat. Rebecca ushers me over to that one black instructor and introduces me as a friend of the family. Of course, we have already met. We have already noticed each other and engaged in the light telepathy necessary in rooms like these, acknowledging that here we are, being careful and softly black. Despite the somewhat offensive ulterior motive of Rebecca's introduction, Robert indulges her and we have a tepid conversation about making plans that neither of us means. At home, Akila is upset. The costume is finished, and while its components were exciting when they were separate and theoretical, on the body it doesn't work. She looks at herself in the mirror and her smile falls. She looks at Eric, whose investment she is not insensitive to, and she pays a few half-hearted compliments, though her embarrassment is palpable, as is ours. We can't be sure if it is shoddy craftsmanship, or the sobering reality of what a costume like this might reasonably look like on a body that is not itself a cartoon.

"It's fine," Akila says, but in the days that follow, it doesn't feel fine, the probiotics and polyethylene glycol doing nothing for my perpetually irritated bowels, though the chronic constipation is eased somewhat by my inability to keep anything down. I resume Call of Duty and introduce that Dutch kid to some friendly fire. I go to the store and buy a few pregnancy tests. I mow some grass and when I see that old white woman watching me through her blinds again, I walk up to her window and look her right in the eye until I realize the lawn mower is veering into the street.

In the morning, I feel sick. I lie in bed all day and get up only to dry heave. At night Rebecca lets herself into my room and tells me to get dressed. She doesn't say where we are going, so I put on a sequin dress and the highest heels I own. When I climb into her truck, she asks me if I'm cold. It is not a question. It is a commentary, but so is this dress. It is meant to say, your ambiguity is tiring. It is meant to say, this is what happens when you leave it up to my interpretation. She puts on the heat and turns the radio to Top 40, and the rotation is always the same, digressive low-frequency capitalism, commercials for tax assistance and sofas and farewell concert promos for the old heads of R&B and quiet storm, but as for the actual music, I don't recognize a single thing. It occurs to me that I have been in Jersey too long. We are in midtown before I realize we are back in the city, and when I look down Sixth, the city actually feels like an island, besieged by hard, yellow water, receding slowly into the loam. And then we are at the hospital. As we take the elevator down to the morgue, I do feel a little stupid about my clothes. When Rebecca offers me a hazmat suit, I am grateful, but determined to remain impassive. Then she opens her locker and brings out an easel, a blank canvas, a steel palette, three paintbrushes, a palette knife, and some yellow, magenta, and cyan. I turn the brush around in my hand and look at the gold lettering on the stem. She opens the door to the morgue.

"The brushes are badger hair. Is that okay?"

"Yes," I breathe, looking at the paints, which are as beautiful as the brushes. Pure, saturated linseed oils. As I'm looking through the supplies, she circles the cadaver and wrings her hands. She already looks like she is tired, but then she puts the radio on and gets her saw. She glances at me a little impatiently, and I realize I, too, am meant to start. I open the easel and set up my canvas. I mix some tertiary colors and make all of them hot, the magenta such a buttery high pigment that I can't bring myself to cool it down. But after the initial rush of establishing my palette, I look at the cadaver and my stomach turns. It isn't the body. It's the audience. Rebecca proceeds as if I am not there, but when I turn to my canvas, I feel her eyes. She tells me to come closer and says to no one in particular: *White, male, eighty-seven, coronary occlusion.* Then she opens the chest and brings out the heart, which is shiny and large and weeping yellow plaque. I do my initial sketch of the body in watered-down cyan, and as I go to fill in the flesh, I find she works faster than I can accommodate. One moment the body is whole, and the next it is turned out like a rind.

The painting is muddy and full of nerves, but inside there is something exact, and after she showers and we drive home, there is a trail of sequins leading to my room. Next time, I put on a T-shirt and jeans. I bring some graphite and a jar of turpentine. I program the radio with a few of my own presets, and Rebecca doesn't protest. As we enter the Holland Tunnel the lights on her dashboard flare. She tells me to ignore it, that her truck has been crying wolf for two years, but as we pull into the hospital, the engine makes a human sound. We put on our suits and I unpack my supplies. She opens the door, and as I'm mixing, she is collecting the large intestine into a silver pan. I get close and she says: *White, male, eighty-nine, prostate cancer.* I do my best not to think too much about it, but it is hard not to take the point of the surgery scars between the rectum and bladder, which is that he tried, and he failed. Of course, this is what Rebecca loves about the work, the stories the bodies tell. She believes the best way to see how a thing is made is to take it apart. She says she was a kid who dismantled all her toys, that it disturbed her mother but her father understood and started buying her things she could assemble from scratch—clocks and cars and model airplanes.

Rebecca smiles at my depiction of a brain that she cuts in half, which, from an aerial view, looks like a spaceship, or a root vegetable. We listen to the radio, and during commercial breaks she tells me more stories in her terse, non sequitur way. Like this: *There was an explosion at the crematorium. Someone forgot to take the pacemaker out.* Or this: *Da Vinci injected molten wax into the cavities of the brain and put the negative image down in ink.* However, I am not inventing the MRI. I am grappling with the tendons of the hand. The masters were masters because their anatomical vocabularies were large, because they understood the lateral, posterior, and anterior aspects of the shoulder, which ultimately helped them depict how Jesus might actually hang on the cross, but there is more language within even the respiratory system than I could ever understand. A week later, Rebecca has an obese Vietnam vet with hyper-inflated lungs (*white, male, sixty-three, asthma attack*), and while she is as strong as a woman who regularly heaves postmortem weight would need to be, she can't move him by herself. I leave my canvas and at her instruction I take the legs, and we move him as one might move a couch up the stairs.

Beyond this, all my joy is underneath my palette knife, the folds of the body more pronounced and so more fun to paint, the palette overwhelmingly Caucasian, and so a little tedious, though inside the body there is room to experiment with blues and dark, cool reds. The cadavers in Rembrandt's paintings were all criminals. The subjects are really the learned men around the corpse. Within my paintings, there is always a half-articulated form of a woman, too mobile to be opaque, craned over the body with forceps in her hand. If she sees herself there, she doesn't mention it. But there are moments when she looks over my shoulder and hums her approval, which of course I resent, but also, a little bit, love.

The second leading cause of death for veterans is suicide, and this is what Rebecca says to me when the next body is young. I bring out my paints, and Rebecca leaves the radio off. After, we both take a shower and we sit in the car with wet hair. We share a cigarette, and two miles from home, we get stranded on the side of the road. While she is on the phone with AAA, she takes a gun out of the glove compartment and asks me to put it in her bag. I turn it over in my hands and try to seem like I haven't seen it before, though because she has seen my paintings, I know she must be aware of the extent to which I have cataloged everything in the house. As it was when I first held it, the gun is crude and prototypical, the barrel thick and square. I unload the cartridge and slide it into her bag. When the tow truck comes, we stand on the shoulder and her hair keeps blowing into her face.

"The painting of your mother is your best one," she says, and I think of the Polaroid camera, of my excitement to capture an unwilling subject while she slept. I think of the photo and its swift revision of a sleeping woman into a dead one. Because in the last days of her life, my mother didn't sleep. There were only prayer circles and essential oils in Tupperware, Seventh-day Adventists with handbells in the living room playing "Power in the Blood" as my father, who wanted to be watching the Yankees game, dabbed myrrh on my mother's skinny brown wrists. The night before my mother killed herself, a deaconess coerced me into taking the F-sharp handbell, and during the segue from "Amazing Grace" to "How Great Thou Art," I looked at my mom and saw clearly her desire to die. As some tone-deaf person began to tell the story of Lazarus, the World Series was playing on a TV upstairs. A ball disappeared in the Bronx and a dead man came forth, and the story always ends there, optimistically, in the middle, with a miracle so high-profile it becomes the catalyst for the Crucifixion, which is technically a fair exchange, man for man, though three days before his death Jesus visited Lazarus again and you have to wonder what he said, if he looked at what Lazarus had done in the meantime and began to question what he was dying for.

When Rebecca and I get home, we start to take off our shoes and we both have kind of a hard time of it, which at first seems coincidental until I feel my own effort to extend this task, and I see that she is doing the same, the silence in the house such a sobering shift from the side of the road that I feel embarrassed just to look at her. Before it becomes ridiculous, she steps out of her shoes. She busies herself with the mail, and I go over and take it out of her hands, though when I look down at it and see that it is Con Ed I don't know what to do. I look at her face and see her irritation, but underneath it something curious and more fixed, and I wrap my arms around her and regret it until she reciprocates, which she takes her time to do, her body shockingly hard as she pulls me in and runs her fingers through my hair, all her ingredients—the formalin and ash and under-eye cream—clarified at close range.

The next afternoon, Eric and I check into a Days Inn. We are both tired and there is something wrong with his back. When we get up to our room, a NARA associate calls him and he spends a while talking about the integrity of a Polynesian tapestry, which apparently has been beset by archival moths. Initially, these phone calls didn't bother me, but as they increase in frequency, I feel these are conversations I am meant to hear, which make apparent his busy-ness and my fortune, to be worthy of this interruption to his day. When he ends the call, we share a four-ounce bottle of gin and I walk on his back for a while and consider the blueprint for the rest of our stay. It occurs to me that maybe he is not interesting and is just older than me, someone who has blown through his budget for failure and landed on the other side with a 401(k). When we have sex it lasts so long that in the middle of it, when it has become less about feeling and more about ETA, we look at each other and call it. I get dressed and tell him I'm going to get some ice, but instead I go to the gym center and lift the barbell as many times as I can. When I return to the room, he is unresponsive on the bathroom floor.

I call reception and an associate comes up and says that it happens all the time. When I climb into the ambulance, I see the EMTs trying to parse our asymmetry. They ask how we are acquainted, what we were doing, and if there were any drugs involved. When they ask for his birthday, I take a stab in the dark. At the hospital, he starts to regain consciousness. I have no choice but to call Rebecca, and when Rebecca arrives, she won't look at me. She asks the nurse a handful of questions in a jargon I don't understand. We stand outside the curtain while Eric provides a urine sample, and the doctor comes around and says syncope is very common, and that because of Eric's low heart rate, he should be careful about rising up too abruptly, which he can do by counting to five before he gets to his feet. After we return to the house, there is no doting. Eric gets out of the car, and Rebecca looks at me in the rearview and tells me that she is going straight to work.

"I didn't mean for this to happen," I say.

"Is there anything that you do mean?"

"This isn't my fault."

"The slogan of your generation."

"Why does it have to be my generation? Why can't it be me, specifically?"

"Because you are not specific," she says. "All of this, it has been done." She looks at me through the mirror and taps a cigarette out of the carton and into her hand. "This isn't serving me anymore."

"What?"

"You have a month, and then I want you out," she says, and then she turns the radio on, and it is a song that we listen to often in the morgue, but there is no recognition on her face. When I get out and watch her drive away, her truck is still making that sound. Inside, Eric and Akila are playing Mario Kart. It is unsurprising that he chooses to be Mario and can't stay on Rainbow Road. As he benefits not at all from Mario Kart's affirmative action and disappears into the dark, I look over at him and I think about the American Library Association certification I found next to his insurance card. I think about the way he looked on the bathroom floor, his open mouth and soft genitals and the veins underneath his pale Lutheran skin, and as a computer-generated Peach and Luigi roll through Moo Moo Farm, I think of how keenly I've been wrong. I think of all the gods I have made out of feeble men. I go to my room and get stuck in a Wikipedia hole about religion on Tatooine. I finish my costume and sit in the dark in my metal bikini, and in the morning I stumble to the bathroom and take the pregnancy test. I am inclined to pray, but on principle, I don't. God is not for women. He is for the fruit. He makes you want and he makes you wicked, and while you sleep, he plants a seed in your womb that will be born just to die.

8

On the morning of Comic Con, Eric comes in from a run and says that the neighbor's dog has been shot. The block is inundated with police. The old woman stands in the street with an upturned doghouse in her arms, and an officer tries to wrestle it away. Beyond them, the dog is covered with a sheet. I watch from my window, and the top of Rebecca's head is briefly visible as she steps outside to retrieve the paper. When I go downstairs, she is removing the sections she doesn't want to read—politics, sports, the horoscope. I take the horoscope and there is a conjunction between Venus and Mars that only the East Coast can see. Outside, a garbage truck tries to maneuver around the police. A harried garbageman dismounts and an officer tells him that he cannot collect the trash today.

Rebecca smoothes a crease from the entertainment section. A starlet is dead. A starlet is breastfeeding on the beach. Her mouth is open and her eyes are closed. Since she asked me to leave, moments come when I think there will be some final, significant word that passes between us, but there is nothing. I want to tell her that I have been painting. I have not made any headway in finding a job or a place to stay, but something is happening on my canvas, whatever soft, human calculus makes a thing alive, gives a painted eye roots and retina and makes it look like it can see. I stay up with a secondhand edition of *Human Anatomy for Artists*, and I start with the cranial bones and keep going until I make it to the teeth. Of course, it isn't the same. I watch her drive off to work, and I think of the damp end of our shared cigarette, of the tiny morgue shower stall and her dainty feet below the curtain, of her bone saw, a discontinued edition designed specifically for a woman's hand. I wake up from a dream where she is trying to put a lung into a jar that is too small, and all day everything smells pickled, though this is probably just the turpentine. I look at cheap studios in Newark and Bensonhurst, but I only have enough money for two months. I only have enough money for a month and an abortion, though on this I go back and forth. I feel unlike myself, spry and nocturnal and inclined to believe that this pregnancy is part of the reason my paintings are any good. Because I can't sleep knowing what is happening inside my body, and when I don't sleep, I paint. I have never been so tired. I have never been so prolific. What if I make the appointment and they ask if I've done it before? What if I am a woman who has to do this twice?

I go to my room and put on the iron bikini and secure the chain around my neck. I look at my stomach in the mirror and feel like there is something inside me already trying to make its way out. Though it is the size of a lentil, I feel a monstrous new level of abdominal antagonism that I cannot solve with ginger root. Rebecca comes into my room with Windex and newspaper. She is half in, half out of her costume, one eye heavily shadowed. Since she asked me to leave, Rebecca lets herself into my room more frequently. Never during the moments I'd like. Acrid, early-morning hours when I haven't yet brushed my teeth. I leave my paintings out, hoping she will see, but she doesn't say anything. Now she comes into the bathroom and begins to clean the mirror. She is careful not to meet my eyes.

I think I could have this baby out of spite. My parents made me on purpose and look what happened. Spite is more sustainable. It gives you something to prove, and what better way to prove yourself than through a child, my personal failure amended by such heroic child-rearing that my kid recognizes patterns even before his skull has fused. A genius child born out of a functional grudge who will accompany me to Eric's funeral, where Rebecca will be shriveled and veiled. When I begin to braid my hair, she watches me, and I try to remain aloof, but I am a little preoccupied with the memory of my first abortion, which I don't think about regularly and occasionally even forget until I open Twitter and have a run-in with a Young Republican. I was sixteen. I could not have been a mother. The women in my family maybe should not have been mothers. This is not so much a judgment as a fact. They were dying inside their own bodies, and now all these dead components are my inheritance.

When the neighbors have all returned to their houses and one of the officers has finally pried the doghouse from the old woman's arms, Akila comes into my room with a hot comb and lets down her hair, which in a month has grown thick and kinky. She is already in her Starfleet uniform, which we purchased from the Party Supply store at the eleventh hour, and which she is not particularly happy about, though as I turn on the stove and put the hot comb to the flame, Akila summons Uhura, practices words in Tamarian, Ferengi, and, of course, Klingon. Over the last couple of months, we have updated her hair care through careful trial and error, even as we were routinely waylaid by suburban convenience stores stocked exclusively with Caucasian shampoos. Once, in Hoboken, we discovered a single bottom shelf with old pomade and congealed Cantu. There were a few trips to Brooklyn, one for oils and one for butters, the homemade and saran-wrapped, the saditty and petroleum-free, Akila's sopping twist-outs transformed by a half percentage point of fall humidity until we forwent the apple cider vinegar and just cracked a few eggs over her head. Now we have a routine: coconut oil, manuka honey, and two firm Bantu knots before bed. As I go through her hair with the hot comb, I imagine its future iterations—the five-dollar ponies and mangled yaki and rainbow Kanekalon and the certainty of a post-breakup big chop, and I wonder where inside this spectrum she will ultimately land. As we are finishing up, Eric comes down the stairs and comments on the smell, but when he sees the source, he seems to gather that it is Something Black, and he is contrite.

He is already in costume, and out of all of us, his physique is closest to the material, a supple inverted triangle that is practically canon, though he has gone for the updated costume, the muted ballistic nylon instead of shiny spandex, which feels less patriotic, but along with his whole working-father vibe is maybe the Captain America you get when the country has, relative to the rest of the world, entered its surly teenage years. As he prepares a cup of tea, I imagine our child, Eric's bone structure, my dysfunctional bowels. I have no doubt that a boy would be beautiful. A girl might have some things to overcome. When Akila is gone, he pours some whiskey into his tea and tries to secure the last component of his costume, a harness he is too drunk to put on. I offer to help and he waves me away, but after a while he gives up and sags into a chair.

He has been this way since his trip to the ER: squirrelly, prone to random displays of machismo, less discreet about how much he drinks. When we met, his drinking always felt situational, a thing he did because we were out. It felt like a necessary preamble, routine, like putting on a sock before a shoe. I should have noticed sooner that some things should not be routine. Looking at him now, it feels impossible that I ever could have missed it. I think about our child again, and this time a slew of predispositions undermine that gorgeous Punnett square. A child with profound narcotic inclinations, with generations of inherited trauma, with questionable brain chemistry and a lifetime of some ceaseless prefrontal seesaw, with my flat, rectangular feet and our mutual taste for disco, which in the year 2045 is likely to be even less cool, Eric's giant umlaut genes meaning nothing if our child grows up in America and drowns in his or her allotted levels of racism-induced cortisol as the earth's sun slowly dies. The only reason I want to tell him is because of the improbability of it, this miraculous fluke that has come about even through the severe limitations of our bodies, a fluke that makes me ill but also dreamy, like something can be different, new. It is not so bad to be an incubator. Everything I eat and drink feels like it amounts to something. Oysters, chocolate, mangos drenched in chili oil, all for a purpose and all excused, an education for the palate I am building with the most acute iterations of sugar and salt. But conversely, it is terrible being an incubator. Everything I do feels like it should amount to something.

As I am getting the harness over Eric's head, Rebecca comes down the stairs in her costume, and like Eric, she has chosen the updated version, fishnets and coochie cutters instead of the jester's romper, though she has stuck with the mallet instead of the baseball bat. Originally, it was meant to be a couple's costume, but when Eric put on the clown makeup, for a night, no one in the house could sleep. Either way, Rebecca's Harley Quinn is so primary, so sullen, it looks best without a counterpart, which is to say that this cosplay does not really suit her, and no cosplay in which she is supposed to be sidekick would. She puts the mallet down on the island, takes a sip of Eric's tea, and

wrinkles her nose. However, she says nothing. She opens the
window and sprays pink dye onto the ends of her pigtails.

Outside, the police are interviewing neighbors and the old
woman is wandering around the yard in a nightgown. With the
window open, the room fills with bleating sirens and neighborhood chatter, but above it all, I hear the old woman wailing. Big,
airless sobs that stop Akila as she is coming back down the
stairs. She goes over to the window and watches with a knowing
reverence. She has mentioned in passing the things that were
lost in the storm, that one of these things was a dog. No doubt
Rebecca is thinking of this as she steers Akila away from the
window and into the car. We are late, and the drive into the city
is already looking bad. Eric slings his shield over his shoulder
and opens the route on his phone; it is red all the way to Thirty-
Fourth Street. When we pile into the car, a police officer is two
houses down, talking with the neighbor who, for the entirety of
my stay, has never said hello. Rebecca waves to the police on
our way out and the officer looks up at her, at the mallet between
her knees, and slowly waves back.

On the road, everyone gets a turn with the aux cord. Eric's
French house and his eyes in the mirror seeking recognition for
deep cuts, Akila's dreary Japanese ska, and Rebecca's mystify-
ing choice of talk radio instead of the music she ostensibly likes,
though folkloric thrash is hardly needed when you are on the
New Jersey Turnpike in the sideways rain. Akila hands me the

aux cord and I go through my phone and try to find something suitable, but all my playlists seem inappropriate—the one I exercise to, the one that is mostly sample-heavy trip-hop I would theoretically have sex to, though most of the time I just end up getting high and looking at unsubtle dystopian memes about how social media is changing the length of the human neck. I flirt briefly with making a statement through my song selection, but I am too old. However, when I see I somehow have half of Phil Collins's *Face Value* downloaded to my phone, it turns out I am not. I put on "In the Air Tonight" and savor the studious readjustments that happen in the car, Akila pointedly turning to her phone, Eric's posture high and rigid as the E-ZPass scans and we cruise through the toll. Of course Rebecca is less obvious, but as we enter the city, she turns to look out of the window and smiles. But after three minutes and fifteen seconds have elapsed, I regret playing the song. It reminds me of how alien their house felt, how quickly it began to feel like mine.

In the city, there is a smell. Hell's Kitchen, a rotting, fungal fruit. Midtown, smelling of mildew and old pecorino. In the two months I've been gone, I forgot that this is what happens in New York when it rains, all the animal and human excretions made into a piping soup. I open the window a little bit and immediately there is a glaze on my face. I have missed it so much, the way the city tilts for all its events. The Puerto Rican Day Parade and the airborne brass of an approaching float. The West Indian Parade and Eastern Parkway's glitter dunes. SantaCon. But today it is Comic Con, and as we approach the convention center, the founders of social awkwardness are climbing from hot fifteen-dollar double-decker buses, towing cases of hardware down Ninth, coming out of the Skylight Diner in their goggles and crinoline skirts, excited to hear about the processes behind their respective cosplays. A man saunters down Tenth in a ball of tinsel and raw cotton, and half of a Final Fantasy VII party is cheering him on. Akila rolls her window down and takes it all in with big eyes. She adjusts her costume and pins on her Command Division badge, and when we stop at a red light, there is a black girl in the car next to us cosplaying as Geordi La Forge. When she sees us, she lowers her visor, leans out of the window, and reaches for Akila's hand. But the light turns green and the car turns onto a side street, her frantic scream of *Live long and prosper!* blunted by city noise.

We have some trouble finding parking. All the garages are full of black SUVs, double-, triple-parked, valets with shiny upper lips coming out with chipped "at capacity" signs, Rebecca navigating the big back end of her truck through midtown with one hand as Eric campaigns for one of three mythic parking spots that were always open between the years of 2002 and 2008. We go to one of the spots and there is a fire hydrant there. Akila leans in between them, her hair already high and wild, and says the first panel starts in ten minutes. Rebecca pulls up to the convention center and tells us to get out, and that she will find a parking spot and catch up later, and I have this feeling, which is 78 percent nausea but 22 percent the dark city ozone opening up to let in a single frond of sun, as Rebecca beckons me over and adjusts the top of my iron bikini, which has been hanging on one hook. She presses her hand into the center of my back and says, *There*, and when I look back at her, she has already turned back to the wheel, already begun hunting for a spot farther uptown as Eric, Akila, and I head into the Comic Con holding pen, a one-hundred-yard tunnel to the Javits Center where a Gundam is Juuling and two pink Power Rangers are pulling cigarettes out of their boots.

At my height, the holding pen is principally a parade of armpits and old CO_2, every mage in sight regretting their cape, the city's moisture pooling into these few dank square feet, everyone rouged and slathered in unicorn spit, a Mario and Luigi arguing about something that happened in Paris and someone's damp scapula pressing against my cheek. You get the feeling that the crowd has become so large and intertwined that the physics are intricate and deeply interior, as if a single load-bearing Darth Maul is holding the whole thing upright. Inside the convention center, the humidity changes form, becomes more human, that specific feeling of smelling a new friend's house quadrupled and condensed, attendees moving to the walls to peel off their ponchos and snap jeweled bracers and web-shooters to their wrists, everywhere you turn someone putting on stockings and rifling through bags full of swag.

It is Saturday. Some hard-core, purple-badged fans have been here since Thursday, and a pair of such fans carve through the crowd with ease, their faces not sleepy so much as smoothed by some profound pleasure that we, as one- to three-day pass holders, see and take as an indication to move aside. There are also babies. A toddler is held above the crowd, Simba-like, and he yawns and pulls at what I assume are noise-canceling headphones. Then he is gone, and as I am trying to find him, for no reason but to see that Space Ghost onesie again, Eric lifts me off my feet and turns me around so that I am facing him, and while this is annoying, I'm also going to miss this when I'm gone, how he used to do this when we were out and about and I wasn't paying enough attention to him—a more rude iteration of snapping one's fingers, forgivable only for the initial jolt, when I am just there in midair. He brings out a Ziploc bag and tells me he is going on a trip. He asks if I want to join, and I decline. He shrugs and eats the gold caps when Akila's back is turned, and then she leads us to the first panel on her schedule. We join hands and move through the crowd as a single, unbalanced chain, Akila at the front, Eric at the back, chewing and holding his shield above his head.

Halfway there, everything is pudding and hands keep coming out of the dark. Because Eric is Captain America. Kids want to take pictures with him, and saying no feels very against the spirit of the thing. He lifts someone's child into his arms, and in the moment before the flash, the kid looks at him and seems uncertain, aware of the pretend, that the eyes behind the mask belong to an archivist from New Jersey. Akila stands off to the side and looks at her watch, which she borrowed from Rebecca specifically for this day. Against the polyester of her Starfleet uniform, the watch is conspicuous, a grown-up piece of jewelry that makes her seem younger, but also like she has the right to be managing us, though Eric is enjoying the attention too much to care. When we get to the panel, we are fifteen minutes late. We stand in the back as an exclusive clip is coming to a close, and Akila pulls one of her eyelashes out. I want to tell her it's okay, but I don't know how to interact with her at this level of frenzy. I thought I had gotten the gist of it the previous week, after someone left an unkind review of her fan fiction regarding some point of canon she'd gotten wrong, and she was, for two days, too depressed to eat, but within this unique environment, her fandom is so violent it feels combustible.

Every person in the room is shiny and taut, breathing through their mouths and looking toward the stage, where the actors, writers, or producers are either very excited or very put off by the energy of the room. *It's my first time*, a voice actor says, and everyone else on the panel laughs. *I watch this show with my mom and I wondered how a lycanthrope can carry a robotic fetus to term*, a fan says, and the room is silent. There is the feeling of conspiracy, glitches in the matrix abundant and kept like an inside joke, the same eight fans who make it to the mics, the villains who gather to admire themselves, universes flattened and set beside each other, long anime sagas truncated by the overlap, nine Gokus and three Kid Flashes, some costumes so professional that for a moment you believe a bandicoot might be able to wear jeans. And all the Harley Quinns. I keep thinking I see Rebecca, but none of them are her. I tap one on the shoulder and when she turns around, she is juggling three grenades filled with laughing gas. An associate at a VR booth wipes a headset down with an antimicrobial napkin and hands it to Akila, and Eric and I look over some paperwork. We confirm that Akila does not have epilepsy or paroxysmal positional vertigo, and Eric makes a show of reading the fine print, which says the VR company isn't liable should something go wrong. When the game has started, Eric turns to me and his pupils are enormous.

"It isn't what you thought it would be," he says, raking his fingers through his hair.

"No," I answer, and he nods and becomes preoccupied with a pretty VR tech who is standing by with a blue bucket until someone yells *Veronica!* and she rushes off with the bucket in tow. As we watch Akila play, it feels like we are witnessing half of a private conversation, the exaggerated physicality that is meant to compensate for what is not actually there, a little daffy, but kind of sweet when you see the moment she truly surrenders to this suspension of disbelief. A VR tech places a gun into her hands, and she shoots it into the air. Around us, the con is still seething, stormtroopers and wizards and gems funneling in from the street and bringing in that copper city air, the body positivity so palpable it feels boastful, like everyone has, for a moment, become the old man in the gym locker room whose scrotum you cannot avoid, though you feel the anxiety in it, that like Akila and her chunky, borrowed watch, everyone is sensitive to the time, a little worried about how Sunday is slowly closing in and so in the throes of a frantic, temporary state, high on some unseen communal steroid and trying to make the most of the day.

A few feet away, the silicon torso of a robot is open to the glitter-ing transistors that form its heart. *A robot's heart is the brain,* Eric mutters into my ear. Someone's baby is crying. An antisep-tic male voice comes from the ceiling and says *willkommen!* A reaper emerges from the crowd with glossy, black wings, and Akila takes off her headset and runs dizzily over. She puts her arms around me and says, *I am so happy right now.* I do my best to be cool about this contact, but it has never happened before, and I pat her awkwardly on the shoulder, terrified that a too-enthusiastic reciprocation will alert her to her error, like the way a white person might raise a jungle cat from birth and be pals for a time until the cat turns five and realizes it is, in fact, a carnivore. If I'm honest, all my relationships have been like this, parsing the intent of the jaws that lock around my head. Like, is he kidding, or is he hungry? In other words, all of it, even the love, is a violence.

Before I go into the booth, I ask Akila to keep an eye on her father. I put on my headset, and at first the only sensation is the warmth of the cushion on my forehead, like a toilet seat that has only recently been vacated, but then I am standing in someone's living room, and then there is a prompt that asks if I would like to watch TV. So I sit on a crudely rendered couch and watch three minutes of *Law & Order: SVU* in a vacated house where there are flowers on the coffee table that I can actually tear apart, which is more thrilling than Mariska Hargitay and Ice-T in the Hamptons interviewing a yuppie who almost certainly put all these women's heads on sticks. In the next demo, I walk around an empty monochrome hospital, and some kind of mist is coming in through the vents. I go into the surgery theater, and a monkey in a blood-spattered apron is taking a Bing Crosby record out of a sleeve. When "White Christmas" comes on, I turn and run. I initiate the last demo, a space walk where I move between six of Jupiter's seventy-nine moons. On the second moon, Europa, which is covered in ice, another explorer emerges from the dark and begins to walk toward me. Above my head, some kind of stellar void is developing. When the explorer reaches me, the sequence ends and when I take the headset off, Rebecca is there with her own headset in her hands. She looks rough, her makeup runny around the eyes.

"Eric is sick," she says dryly, and when I turn, Eric is a few booths down, puking into one of those blue buckets. While he retches, Akila holds his shield and checks her watch.

"Shrooms," I say, and Rebecca nods. Her hands are shaking. "Are you okay?"

"Perfect," she says, as Akila hands off the shield. She and Akila slip wordlessly into the crowd, and I go over to Eric, who is in the recovery area having some juice. I find some loose Tums in my purse and give them to him.

"What, you don't like me anymore?" he says after a long silence. The way he says it, it's as if some nicer half of a conversation has already occurred, and now we are here. He gets up to go to the bathroom and I follow him inside. He turns and gives me a look, but his privacy, and the privacy of the Aquaman at the urinal, means nothing to me.

"I don't know if I ever liked you," I say, and bathroom acoustics being what they are, the declaration is magnified and that much more unkind, which makes me feel bad until I see that he is missing a shoe, and I feel it anew, this terrible disappointment in myself that I am happy to take out on him. He is the most obvious thing that has ever happened to me, and all around the city it is happening to other silly, half-formed women excited by men who've simply met the prerequisite of living a little more life, a terribly unspecial thing that is just what happens when you keep on getting up and brushing your teeth and going to work and ignoring the whisper that comes to you at night and tells you it would be easier to be dead. So, sure, an older man is a wonder because he has paid thirty-eight years of Con Ed bills and suffered food poisoning and seen the climate reports and still not killed himself, but somehow, after being a woman for twenty-three years, after the ovarian torsion and student loans and newfangled Nazis in button-downs, I too am still alive, and actually this is the more remarkable feat. Instead I let myself be awed by his middling command of the wine list.

"I didn't mean that," I say, mostly to make myself feel better, but also because despite everything, it's true. I did like him, once. When we were theoretical. When we were at the top of the coaster and the wind was in his hair.

"It's fine if you did." He seems to notice now that his shoe is missing. "I was careless with you."

"No, I liked that," I say, and he smiles.

"Yeah. What was that about?"

"I don't know. Probably something to do with my dad."

"Good." He laughs. "I mean, not *good*. I don't know why I said that."

"Hey. Have you ever thought about going to a meeting or something?" I say, and he takes off his mask and looks at me.

"I'd like to be alone if that's okay," he says, and I go back out onto the floor and wander around as the night is coming in, all the Saturday attendees wilted and missing pieces of their costumes, toting around swords and crystals and polyethylene toys.

A happy black family comes up to me and asks if they can take a picture with me. *A black Leia!* the mother says, so excited that I actually try to get the smile into my eyes, though when they scroll through the pictures, I can see from their faces that the pictures have not turned out well. I wander around for a while and end up in Artists' Alley, a section of the convention I saw on the website and assumed would be composed of signing tables for comic book conglomerates, but which is so much more— sexy, modern portraits that have been reproduced from their original graffiti; sleek, hyperrealist fan art; painters working on the floor, pausing to stow their brushes while they make a sale; homemade zines and tarot cards; graphic novelists struggling with mobile card readers and strongboxes as attendees press their noses to their newly purchased canvas prints. Of course I am envious, but as I am coming to the end, there is a booth with the coolest prints I have ever seen. The artist, a very normal-looking black woman in a wool sweater, looks up from her ice cream and tells me that her graphic novels are loosely based around her quest to find adequate psychotherapy. I open one of the books to a random page and there is a spread of dark, residential road. And I don't know if it is the texture of the pavement, or the single yellow window suspended above the trees, but there is a feeling in my chest, and for a moment I can't breathe.

"This is really beautiful. I'm sorry," I say, so determined to put this feeling behind me that I leave the convention center entirely and remain outside until Akila, Eric, and Rebecca are ready to go home. On the way to the car, Rebecca mentions that she has had to park a ways uptown, and after we get on the A and take it all the way to Fifty-Ninth, she mentions that there was a minor accident, though when we get to the car, the front is smashed in, and two of the windows are gone. We don't talk about it. Instead, we pile into the car and begin removing the less comfortable parts of our costumes, and by the time we make it home, there is an increased police presence in the neighborhood and the car is filled with smoke. All night, everyone has a cough.

When everyone is asleep, I go out to get some air, and I look up the average cost of diapers, but even this is an optimism I can't afford, as it is unlikely any child of mine would have normal intestinal health.

It is only when I get up to go back inside that I look across the street and see the old woman watching me, standing in her yard with a leash in her hand. Once I am back in my room, I look out of the window and she is still there. I close my curtains and look up the graphic novelist. I find her LinkedIn, Twitter, and Instagram, and I am shocked that she is the same person on all three. Four years at RISD, and then a stint in a posh mental institution before she began her series. On a badly produced podcast about how to handle getting stiffed for freelance work, she says that when she was in the hospital, her assigned therapist kept falling asleep, and when I hear her laugh, the way it is big and ugly like mine, I go to the contact form on her website and send an effusive and apologetic letter. In the morning, Rebecca comes into my room and begins to clean the windows. Before she leaves, she tells me that I should find a way to tell Akila that I'm leaving.

It hadn't occurred to me that I would need to do this, but when I take my Captain Planet mug from the cupboard and make the coffee, all I can think is, *Of course*. I sit in the dark and try to figure out a nice way to tell Akila that I am abandoning her, that her father and I don't really have sex anymore, that her mother has evidently had enough. I know her life has been shaped principally by the sudden departure of people she trusts, and I am not going to buck the trend. I take the train to Dumbo to interview for an internal communications gig I don't want, and the entire time I am wondering who will do Akila's hair.

The next day, I call Akila out of school, and she does not seem particularly enthusiastic. She says she has a test and asks if anyone has died. I assure her that everyone is safe, and then I pressure her into a day of hooky. We take the bus to Garden State Plaza, and I give her one hundred dollars. She squints at the cash and asks why it is damp, and this is the kind of attitude she has for most of the day. I let her take the lead on which stores we visit, and each time she cuts one cursory circle around the perimeter and darts back out. Though I assumed any Goth-lite accessory would do, she seems to have no distinct taste in clothing, though she lingers on a pair of rain boots at Dick's Sporting

Goods. We go into Macy's and she plucks a bland, shapeless dress from the rack and tells me that it looks like something I might wear. I try not to let it hurt my feelings, but she does it again at Mango, and then at the Gap. I relent and try one of the dresses on, and it actually doesn't look too bad. Then I notice a yellow crust on the mirror and feel sick. In the mall bathroom, I throw up for a while, and when I come out, Akila is much more agreeable.

She puts her phone away, and we walk silently through the mall until she decides that she would like to buy some legitimate underwear. At her age, I felt such shame about my breasts that I refused to even acknowledge them. I wore a bathing suit underneath my clothes to flatten them, but because of an extremely nosy group of West Indian elders in my church, whose sole purpose was monitoring the sexual development of young women in the congregation, I didn't get away with it for long. In the fitting room, my mother attempted to stuff my breasts into a cute, age-appropriate bra, but my body had ceased to be the sort of hard, inchoate thing you might call cute. Instead, it had, at thirteen measly years, become soft and serious, visible to men and in need of copious support. And while Akila has the typical ambivalence about her own body, she is not like this. She invites me into the fitting room, tries on a few bras, and asks me what I think. *Good*, I say, trying to locate the most sensitive word. I help her adjust the straps, and she shrugs and slips them into her purse. It happens so quickly that by the time we are out of the store, the window in which I could have said something has closed. In the next store, she does it again, and no explicit plan is made, but soon we are moving in tandem, sliding bracelets and sample perfumes into our purses and stowing what we can in our boots. After an hour, we stop at Orange Julius, and we look at each other and laugh.

"Do you do this often?"

"Sometimes." She turns the cup around in her hands. "You're leaving," she says matter-of-factly, like she has already spent some time with the news.

"Yeah. I'm sorry."

"Don't be," she says, and then we slip into a movie, but it is already halfway through, and I can't really make sense of it. Everyone in the theater is crying, and when I look at Akila, she is crying, too. On the way to the bus, we argue half-heartedly about what we think the movie meant. For the rest of the ride, we are silent, and when we get to the house, Eric and Rebecca are not home. As Akila is looking for her keys, a patrol car pulls up behind us. As it has become common in the last week for a car or two to make rounds at night, I assume it will proceed around the cul-de-sac, but when two officers exit the car, this assumption reveals itself to be mostly hope. *Evening*, one of the officers says, and when I say it back, it sounds so weak that I clear my throat and say it again, though the second time it sounds worse, forceful, and I feel the error in this overcorrection, the officers silent, recalculating.

I should know better. The effort to appear casual is never a casual act, but in front of the police I don't know how I can be expected to act like myself. I don't know how not to assume the posture of defense. I look at the officers, and then at all the lit windows around the cul-de-sac, and in one of the windows, I see the old woman's face. I ask if there is a problem, and this time

I don't try to correct for the tremor. But when they ask if I live in the house, I hesitate, and Akila crosses her arms and says that she does, her tenor markedly less reverent than mine. One of the officers turns to look at her, and I can feel the impending spiral of this exchange, my fear of the officers' increasing proximity tempered somewhat by the oddness of our shared incredulity at Akila's departure from the script. I can't tell if it is defiance or if she simply doesn't know the words. I step in front of her and tell her to go around the back. But she won't, and there is a part of me that sees her ease, her self-possession, and is frustrated for what she hasn't been told. But when I see how she is resolute, casual in her claim of what is hers, I am envious. When the officers ask me to show ID, I look for my license, but my hands are shaking and my purse is full of stolen perfume. *This is my home,* Akila says, and I know that the moment between when a black boy is upright and capable of speech and when he is prostrate in his own blood is almost imperceptible, due in great part to the tacit conversation that is happening beyond him, that has happened before him, and that resists his effort to enter it before it concludes. I know that the event horizon is swift because of the gulf between the greeting and the pavement, but in real time, as they press Akila to the ground, every second is long.

As it happens, everyone involved is denied some kind of dignity, the officers' brute force sincere and absurd, the exertion rendering them small, and Akila, surprised and clumsy and afraid, so conspicuously a child that I run over without thinking and try to get them off, the whites of her eyes bright in the porch light before an officer lifts me into his arms and presses me down into the grass and says *Stop resisting*, which my ears receive as Greek but also as déjà vu, because not even in what is feasibly my last moment can I be free from the internet and the digital hall of mirrors in which orders are issued unironically to dying women and men. When I stop resisting, it is because I can no longer hear Akila's voice. For a moment, I only hear geese, and somewhere, an ice cream truck. But then Rebecca is calling out from the end of the driveway, and when I turn my head, her truck is parked sideways in the middle of the street, smoking, and she is running in her scrubs and Docs, waving her arms and saying words I can't make out. The officers' retreat is almost coordinated. Rebecca hurries over to Akila, and as she gets to her feet, the officers straighten their clothes.

"We wanted to touch base with the owner of the house. Per the incident earlier this week."

"The dog."

"Yes, ma'am." Akila gets up and goes around the back, and when I try to go with her, she pushes me away. "Do you know Ms. Moynihan?"

"Not well, no."

"Do you have any firearms inside the house?"

"Of course not," Rebecca says, and our eyes meet briefly before I go around the back.

Inside, Akila has shut herself in her room. I knock on the door, and when she answers, her lip is bleeding. When I draw her attention to it, she is surprised. *I can't feel it,* she says, covering it with her hand, and when I get the first aid kit and tend to the cut, she says it again in a small, disembodied voice.

"I shouldn't have talked back," she finally says. "I feel—" She pauses, collects herself. "I feel really stupid."

"No, there's nothing we could have done. It was always going to go that way."

"Is that supposed to make me feel better?" she says, her voice low, tight. I remember when my parents tried to tell me this, the only time in their miserable marriage they were ever united. It must be strange for every black kid, when their principal authority figures break the news that authorities lie. Ironically, I didn't believe them. I had to find it out for myself.

"You're not going to feel better about this," I say. "You're going to feel angry, for a long time, and that's your right."

"Okay," she says. "Okay. I don't want to talk about it anymore." We sit in silence for a while, and then we resume our video game—a collaborative multiplayer where we have to prepare burgers for a ravenous fast-food crowd. But we are out of sync. She can't get the pickles down in time and I keep dropping the mayonnaise. As the level reloads, the screen goes dark and reflects our faces back to us, and though we continue to play, our reflections, our stricken expressions, remain in the room. During a level interlude, I turn and put my arm around her and she accepts my embrace, briefly, before we turn back to the game.

It is the first night we all have dinner together. Eric and Rebecca watch Akila as she eats, and she takes a few bites and asks if she can go back to her room. Eric tries to follow her, and Rebecca simply places a hand on his arm. Later, I try to paint. When I can't, I sit in front of the mirror and do a quick graphite study of my face, and for the first time in my life, there I am. Or, at least, something about it is recognizable, but the timing is bad. Because among the dumb, insufficient platitudes I might offer to Akila or myself is the truth. And the truth is that when the officer had his arm pressed into my neck, there was a part of me that felt like, all right. Like, fine. Because there will always be a part of me that is ready to die.

Later, Rebecca lingers in my doorway until I motion for her to come in. After two months of her pointed intrusions, this propriety feels absurd. She closes the door and glances at the two garbage bags where I have packed all my things. She sits on the floor and removes her shoes, leans back against the door.

"You're okay."

"Yeah," I say, and when I look over at her, her eyes are bright and still.

"Sometimes, I hoped something bad might happen to you." She laughs. "Isn't that monstrous?"

"Doesn't matter," I say, and as the room darkens, her face slackens and becomes novel, almost inanimate. I draw it quickly before all the light is gone, and once it is night, we sit in silence until I am asleep. When I wake up, she is stretched out on the floor. But something is wrong. I go to the bathroom and when I turn on the lights, I am covered in blood. My first impulse is to wash my hands, but as I'm doing it, I see myself in the mirror and stop. There isn't enough toilet paper, and when I reach for the showerhead, I feel the beginning of a terrible abdominal cramp. I wake up Rebecca, but none of the words that come make any sense. I am both grateful and horrified to find that she wakes up promptly to a fully alert state, like a grim little computer, and after she clocks the bloodied pajamas in my arms, she gets me clean sweatpants and ushers me downstairs and into the truck with a box of sanitary pads. *The seats*, I say, which is the first coherent thing I've said since waking up, and she pulls out onto the road and gives a dry, mirthless laugh. Dawn is breaking and the road and sky are in and out as we drive, the dark behind my eyes softer and warmer than the car and the AC that Rebecca has directed right onto my face, but in the dark, I don't have to feel it, and I don't have think about it, what is happening inside of me.

As she is helping me through the parking lot, I can hear the day becoming whole. Traffic and avian chatter and wind in the trees. We enter urgent care, Rebecca lowers me into a smooth, green chair, and I remember that I don't have health insurance. I close my eyes again, and when I open them, she is doing paperwork, writing my birthday in her sloppy, right-handed script. I don't ask her how she knows. I know I have been vetted and carefully observed, and I know Rebecca does not like to be surprised. But when she fills out the details of my medical history, sends the paperwork back with her credit card, almost as if it is nothing, I feel held.

The bleeding hasn't stopped. When a nurse comes for me, I'm embarrassed to get up. There is a spot on the chair, and as they are taking me away, I look back and Rebecca is trying to clean it up. It happens quickly. A paper gown and an intake bracelet that is too tight. A Wyeth painting mounted above a box of purple gloves. The sweatpants, inside out and heavy with blood. Cold jelly and the murmur of the sonogram. I can't help feeling that the painting is inappropriate. It depicts a woman crawling through tall, brown grass. The woman was Wyeth's neighbor, and she was suffering from a neurodegenerative disease that impacted her ability to walk. This painting is hanging in the room where a doctor tells me that the baby is dead and the tissue will need to be cleared.

They give me a pill to soften my cervix and then a light sedative. The nurse calls it a *twilight sleep*. As she walks me through what will happen during the uterine aspiration, I can't shake the feeling that she once served me at an IHOP in Flatbush, and while it's possible a lot has changed for her since then, I feel sort of uneasy as she explains the procedure and palms the speculum. When she asks me what I do, I tell her that I don't do anything. But as they are turning on the machine, it feels important that I be earnest, and I grab her arm and tell her that actually, I am an artist. It is an embarrassing declaration, even as the room is going dark, but when I wake up and they provide me with a diaper, the declaration feels no different from a theoretical child, a thing I've cultivated mostly in my mind, cautiously, desperately. A sunlit dream where I do better, where there is no father and my daughter and I move upstate and sometimes I yell at her while helping her with her homework, but ultimately we are pals, and she is someone I can talk to, ill-tempered and serious and leaving bowls of cold cereal around the house, off to kindergarten with noisy, ornate hair, because like black mothers everywhere, I will be required to overdo it with the barrettes. And maybe it is not all great and in my single motherhood my bandwidth is shot with work and child-rearing and trying to get laid. Maybe I bring too many men into her life and she wishes she knew who her dad was, and I tell her that I don't know, the months in Jersey like a brief, sunlit seizure. Maybe she is too much like me, too much like my mother, teetering silently on some horrific precipice in her teenage years until she comes out the other side as the woman I couldn't be, a woman with good credit and hope and who is terrifying in her conviction to be whatever it is she wants to be.

"I didn't even want to be a mother," I say when Rebecca and I are almost halfway home.

"Neither did I," she says, and when we pull into the driveway and Eric walks past the kitchen window, I feel it anew. I fiddle with my seat belt and the AC, and Rebecca allows me the pretense. I would like to take a shower and bleed in private, but the hard, ceramic light of the afternoon changes the house, makes it feel opaque, too fixed to accommodate what has happened quickly and with significant carnage. In a year, maybe this will be okay. But today I wear an adult diaper and there is no god, no child, no hypothetical in which there is a farmhouse at the end of all that crunchy, brown grass. There is only the recycling and the white clapboard, dappled in sun.

Rebecca and I sit in the car for an hour, and once we are inside, she remains close by. I haven't asked her to do this, and in fact, I feel some resentment at her presumption, but mostly there is this unspoken agreement that in the wake of this bloody and preposterous thing, everything else can be put aside. We orbit each other wordlessly for days, chamomile and ibuprofen appearing on my dresser out of nowhere, like the old days, when we were more tentative, and the house felt like it had a finite amount of air. Rebecca leaves me muesli and Percocet and I go on StreetEasy and look for studios in Bedford Park and Gravesend, and when I do a Google Street View of one of the apartments, it is just an enormous crater in the ground. *Newly Renovated!* it says, and so I move to Craigslist, and there are a few that look somewhat hospitable to women, but for each one there is a caveat, requirements that potential roommates be "fun" or into the holy spirit, florid descriptions of Orangetheory and how close everyone in the house already is.

In the week it takes me to heal, I go through a few boxes of thick, hospital-grade sanitary napkins, and in general feel like I am being kept as a new vampire's main source of food, hard, dark clots of blood in the first days and then a bloodbath so relentless I feel godlike just to be alive. And on the day it stops, I get the internal communications job I interviewed for a few weeks before, a job

I actively do not want but that offers paid sick leave, health insurance, and a free mattress, the hiring manager a black woman who halfway through the call tells me plainly to negotiate my package before I say yes, and so I say a number, about five grand more than I feel I deserve, and she simply says, *Very good.*

While I am waiting for the paperwork to come through, Rebecca and I take even more incremental steps toward each other until we are basically moving through these last days with our fingers linked, as stiffly as this can possibly be done, our adjacency embarrassing but somehow necessary, even as I am certain she is relieved the child didn't live. Because in the moments we are closest, there is always a caveat, always a clock running out, and nothing can be purely sweet. I wake up in the morning and think for a moment that I am someone happier and then I remember where I am.

Then we move through the day side by side, and I feel like the exception, like there is some vestigial organ we share that is essentially a second tongue, our language furtive and crude and articulated only in private, this feeling in both of us, that we are building something out of glass. At times, it feels awful, like it is only this way because there is an expiration date. I go into the city and I watch a broker in a tracksuit flush a newly installed toilet. I get stuck underground while another broker is waiting for me in Forest Hills. On the F, a rat scurries over my feet. And of course, there are babies everywhere. Haggard parents hefting carriages up and down the subway stairs. When I get back to New Jersey, there is an ache between my legs.

I unpack my paints and I stretch a canvas. I take my time with the gesso, thin it with water to make sure there are no lumps. I lay down a cool background color, and while it dries, I feel myself becoming anxious, too particular about the state of my brushes, which, during the length of my short but generative pregnancy, became stiff with old paint. I sit in the dark and think of the doctors who performed the procedure, and I imagine them at home, spanking their children and smoking cigarettes. I wonder if it is common to ask a patient what she does as the twilight sleep begins, if it functions as a truth serum, or a moment in which patients think of what they would like to be doing with their lives and lie. I want to feel that when I said I was an artist, it wasn't a lie. But when I try to paint, I am out of sync, still used to the rhythm I kept in my pregnancy-induced insomnia, when I stowed jars of oily artichoke hearts under my bed for delirious painting jags that went on until dawn, which I described, in great detail, to a child who did not yet have ears. *Orange, yellow, pink.* I do it now almost automatically, and when I catch myself, I feel angry.

I go down into the kitchen at dawn and fill a bowl with artichoke hearts, and I move through the house and select a few things I would like to take with me: Akila's Captain Planet mug, Eric's Bumblebee Unlimited vinyl, and a half-used bottle of Rebecca's ginger and bergamot perfume. I wrap the breakables in a pair of jeans, and at nine, I haul my bags to Rebecca's truck. The morning is blank and sullen, and the AC is dead. We stop for coffee, and the back of Rebecca's shirt is dark with sweat. I try to make small talk and she puts on her sunglasses and says *Yeah, yeah,* though I did not ask a question and there is no sun. On the radio, every station is muddied by the echo of an approximate frequency, and it is only when we reach Crown Heights and Rebecca kills the engine that I hear a voice say, *Tonight only,* before we climb the stairs to my apartment, a sixth-floor walk-up with a brand-new toilet and too-friendly cat. I am happy to find that my roommate, who has texted only to ask if I am allergic to nuts, is not home. Rebecca goes through the apartment and turns all the faucets on, and after I am done spraying the perimeter of my room with Raid, I come out and find she has disassembled them all, the chrome, rubber, and silicone coils laid out neatly on damp paper towels. *Your water pressure is terrible,* she says, and I am tempted to say that she should've paid me more. I am tempted to ask why her sporadic payments included so many coins. After, the water pressure is better, but I cannot help feeling that any attempt to improve this situation, the indelible ruin of New York real estate, is absurd. My new full bed, which has been waiting at the bottom of the stairs for two days, already has something of a smell. It takes us a while to get it up the stairs, and a couple of times Rebecca falls. We don't bicker, but after, we wash our faces violently, and then we share a cigarette outside. She touches the inside of my wrist, and immediately I feel like I might cry. *Don't tell him,* I say, and when we are back in the apartment, we share a small bottle of vodka I stole from the Marriott minibar and I use my roommate's record player to listen to the vinyl, which, despite Eric's preservation method, has been warped by heat. And so as we drink, we are constantly adjusting the needle, though when it is dark, we give up and let it skip, the interval long enough to justify the return and render it almost invisible, though on some level we are aware of the drone and how we have begun to mirror its signature as we talk, the content of our words increasingly illegible as we move around each other like two magnets of identical charge. I hold this frustration inside myself until we are once again on opposite sides of the room, and I say *Don't move*, too loudly. When she obeys, I think we are both surprised. But immediately after, there is an expectation in the air, the language that we share now whittled down to the essential vocabulary, to soft, yearning words, conjugations that are ardent and hard. I tell her to get undressed, to take her time, partly because I am getting my oils together and partly because I want to spend time with the body that has been showing itself to me, for months, in small, insolent degrees. When she is undressed, I still feel the old impulse to compare, but otherwise her body is like a dagger, like the body of a woman who is in the business of sending off the dead. And this is how she holds herself, like a person uninterested by her own anatomical drama, her bearing unselfconscious, indifferent. It feels like a challenge. I mix my paints, deep, quaternary colors, rust, ash, dirty turquoise, and then I take her face into my hands and pull her mouth back with my fingers so that I can see her teeth.

When she doesn't protest, I arrange her into the position I want, one limb at a time, until she is taut. There is no coy, lingering touch, though I can feel her expectation of me when I press an arch into her back, and I am struck by the soft knots of her spine, the way her body feels mutable, her age a vivid, enviable thing. I feel her commitment as she rises up onto her toes, and I have made the pose demanding on purpose, but as I collect my palette and take my place on the floor, it feels overly punitive, and I am not sure if after all of this, I will even be able to paint it faithfully. But then I see her seriousness, the way she remains as she was arranged, and the work begins on its own, her nakedness gorgeous data that in translation does not feel salacious. As we work, the light changes in the room, and the painting becomes a composite of contradictory shadows. When I turn it around to show her, she comes down onto her heels and puts a hand up to her mouth. *Oh*, she says, and then she takes a while to put on her clothes. I look away to give her privacy, but also because it is suddenly hard to watch, the indulgence so close to the aftermath that it feels indecent to watch her tie her shoes. But when this is done, there is no ceremony. There are no words, and she lets herself out.

When she is gone, I stow the painting in a place I am unlikely to notice it regularly, and for a moment, I feel like I've forgotten how to be alone. It is not that I want company, but that I want to be affirmed by another pair of eyes. The acceptable interval for which I can be embarrassed for what I said to the doctors has passed, but I still think about it for weeks, what I meant when I said I was an artist. I think about the painting in the clinic and the canvas fibers curled beneath the oil. All the raw materials that are gathered and processed into shadow and light. The pigments drawn from sand and Canterbury bells, the carbon black drawn from fire and spread onto slick cave walls. A way is always made to document how we manage to survive, or in some cases, how we don't. So I've tried to reproduce an inscrutable thing. I've made my own hunger into a practice, made everyone who passes through my life subject to a close and inappropriate reading that occasionally finds its way, often insufficiently, into paint. And when I am alone with myself, this is what I am waiting for someone to do to me, with merciless, deliberate hands, to put me down onto the canvas so that when I'm gone, there will be a record, proof that I was here.

ACKNOWLEDGMENTS

This book wouldn't have been possible without the support of my family and friends. Thank you to Mom, Dad, and Sam for your light and encouragement. To Doug, for giving me the first book I ever loved. To Daimion, for giving me my first sketchbook. To Evan, for being an incredible partner and friend. Every day I am in awe of your kindness. To the literary journals who championed my work when I was just beginning to write. To New York University's MFA program, where I met friends and mentors who lifted me up and helped me keep going. To the people in my cohort who became family and made me a better writer and person. To Katie, Zadie, Jonathan, Deborah, Hannah, and John for seeing me and pushing me. To Ellen and Martha for your fierce advocacy. To Kish, for your care and brilliance. To Gaby, for your warmth and savvy. To Melissa for this beautiful cover. To the whole Picador team for your support and enthusiasm. Thank you all for helping me make this dream a reality.